I

Novels By Morgan Stang

The Bookshop and the Barbarian

Murder at Spindle Manor

The Bartram's Maw Series

Book 0.5: *The Wolf and the She-Bear*

Book 1.0: *She Topples Giants*

Book 2.0: *She Courts Darkness*

Book 2.5: *The Spider and the Scribe*

Book 3.0: *She Heralds the End*

The Bookshop and the Barbarian

A Cozy Fantasy Novel

Morgan Stang

I cannot promise you a life of sunshine;
I cannot promise riches, wealth or gold;
I cannot promise you an easy pathway
That leads away from change or growing old.
But I can promise all my heart's devotion
A smile to chase away your tears of sorrow;
A love that's ever true and ever growing;
A hand to hold in yours through each tomorrow.

—Mark Twain, "These I Can Promise"

Chapter 1

Maribella Buys a Bookshop

Maribella Waters arrived at her newly purchased bookshop to find it infested with incredibly rude goblins.

But we're getting ahead of ourselves. First she had to get there. And how did she get there? Pig wagon. She rolled into the town of Leafhaven in the back of a wagon filled with pigs. If that seems like a crude or lowborn or unappealing method of travel, then you should take a good hard look at your prejudices.

Maribella found the town of Leafhaven to be a quaint one, with little quaint cobbled streets and houses with quaint arched roofs. Chimneys churned out smoke and slightly swinging lamps hung above doorways. Cats prowled down alleyways and dogs observed the world from comfortable pillows at windows. It smelt like a good place, tucked away as it was right up against the edge of a forest with beautiful maple trees just starting to turn their colors.

There was also an abundance of pumpkins, Leafhaven being a pumpkin town, of course. Pumpkins sat on porches and window ledges and up and down streets. Why Leafhaven wasn't called Pumpkinhaven I'll never know, but it was a great opportunity and now it's gone.

Edgar the pig farmer brought his wagon to a stop in the center of town on a street called Main Street. It was called Main Street because the people of Leafhaven weren't very imaginative.

"Yar," called Edgar. "Here we be, wee lass. Leafhaven at last. 'Twas a fine journey with you, 'twas."

"Indeed it 'twas. I mean...was," said Maribella. "Thank you very much for letting me come along. I wish I had more to pay you, but I've got to make a little stretch a lot."

"Yar, you've already overpaid me as it is. Here, I made this for you during the trip. I enjoy whittling, I do, and sometimes I'll take to whittling while sitting idle for a long spell, like on long trips such as this. It's a pig."

Edgar handed Maribella a chunk of misshapen wood that looked nothing like a pig.

"Oh..." she said.

"Yar, I know. 'Tis awful, it is. Perhaps whittling while on a bouncy wagon ride isn't the best idea in the world." He rubbed at some bandaged cuts on his hands. "If only there was something I could do while sitting about for long periods of time, like on these very trips."

"Well actually, I just bought a bookshop and—"

"Yar, if only there was something," said Edgar, and he was already on his way to the next town, shaking his head and looking at his empty hands.

Maribella huffed and hefted her pack of only possessions onto her back. "*Well* then," she said, watching the wagon of pigs leave. The pigs looked back.

There go some mighty fine pigs, she thought.

At least she might've thought that. How would I know? I can't read minds. I can only guess through context clues as to what anyone thought at any given time. The events of this story are completely, totally, absolutely true without any question or doubt. But who knows what any one person was really thinking at the moment? She could have also thought, *I wonder if Edgar overcharged me*, or *I need a bath as soon as possible*, or *I'd like get a pet pig now.*

In the future, I won't dwell on the various possibilities of what people thought at any given time, and thoughts shall simply be conveyed as if they were the absolute truth. To settle the argument between us now, let us simply agree that as Maribella stood there, wistfully watching the wagon of pigs roll away, she thought:

I'll never look at a plate of ham the same way again.

Maribella got her bearings. She observed Main Street and studied all the people going to and fro about their business, and they seemed like very fine people. They didn't look diseased at all. On the contrary, there was a fairly healthy balance of young men and women who seemed to live productive lives, and the elderly who were well-taken care of. There were also many playful children. This was all a good thing in Maribella's eyes. The town of Leafhaven wasn't a large town, true, but it was clear that Main Street was the place to be.

She tried to stop a child running along pushing a hoop with a stick. "Excuse me," she said. "Do you know where the Cozy Q—"

"Tra la la!" sang the child unhelpfully. "I have a stick and hoop!" And then he ran away.

"What a dreadful child," said Maribella.

She walked along until she found an older gentleman smoking a pipe while leaning up against the rail to the front porch of a shop that sold paper lanterns. "Good day there, fine sir," said Maribella with a smile. "Would you happen to know where the Cozy Quill B—"

"*Who's it with the what now, what's it?*" snapped the man, working his gums.

"Oh, my," said Maribella, hurrying along. The last thing she wanted was to get into some kind of fight with a confused old man upon first arriving in town.

She explored Leafhaven some more, and we should all be happy that the next several people she talked to were as kind as could be, and were glad to point her along toward the Cozy Quill Bookshop, which was situated right on Main Street just down the way a bit.

Maribella smiled while standing in front of the building. It was a lovely place, if a little dilapidated, but Maribella never was one to mind things that needed a bit of work. The place had been sitting empty for a good twenty years, after all. It was larger than she was expecting, standing two stories high with a tiny tower at the top. A display window area was next to the front door, and these windows pressed outward a bit so that choice wares could be set up right there for all to see. The wood walls needed a paint job, and the roof needed tending to, but other than that it was a fine building (it should be said, however, that there was a depressing lack of pumpkins whatsoever anywhere near the place).

Maribella readied the keys that had been sent to her from the Baron, but was surprised to find the door ajar.

"That's not good," she said.

It smelled old and dusty inside, but thankfully not damp. There were no dripping sounds, and no immediate signs of water damage. That had been Maribella's biggest concern.

She smiled as she entered the main shop floor. It took up most of the building with its vaulted ceiling, but what made her smile the most were the rows and rows of books that came with the shop.

"This place was a steal," she whispered. She was alone, so she didn't need to whisper, but she was still in a bookshop and so she felt the need to.

Besides, it felt like she was unearthing an ancient, long lost tomb. The Cozy Quill was old and forgotten, with spiderwebs and dusty shelves and creaky old floorboards. The light from the front windows failed to properly illuminate the place, so it almost felt downright spooky.

And then Maribella turned a bookshelf corner near the back of the room and realized she actually *wasn't* alone. A gang of goblins had taken up residence in the bookshop while it was abandoned.

She could have stumbled across any number of woodland creatures and fables residing in her bookshop. Kobolds, imps, pixies, blue slimes, trolls, gnolls, bugbears, hobgoblins, etc. But no, these particular creatures were goblins.

The astute readers will now realize we've come full circle in our introduction to Maribella's story. All other readers should flip back to the first line of this book, read it again, then come back here.

So why didn't we just start with Maribella discovering this gang of goblins residing inside her property? Excellent question. Everything before this point was backstory regarding the wooden pig that Edgar the pig farmer had whittled for Maribella. That's an important item that will have relevance later, so don't forget about it.

Now Maribella had never met a goblin before, but she had seen plenty of drawings and had read plenty about them, and these seemed like your perfectly typical goblins. They were all about two to three feet tall, and had green skin with squashed oval heads. They wore tiny clothing with adorable daggers tucked into their belts, and metal bits and other barbaric decorations pierced their giant, pointed ears. Big bones that were either weapons or dinner leftovers were strewn about the place. It was a mess.

These goblins, as fearsome as they appeared, behaved in the most non-fearsome manner possible. They were all asleep.

Maribella cleared her throat. "Ahem. Excuse me," she said, and then gently nudged the nearest goblin's foot. "*Excuse me.*"

Some of the goblins stirred but didn't wake. They snored and made little sounds in their gentle sleep that would have been calming in any other situation.

"I said *excuse me!*" cried Maribella. More goblins stirred. None of them addressed her. "This is my bookshop, I'm sorry to say, and I've got to settle in and get it ready to open up. I can't do that with you lot here. I'm afraid you're going to have to find residence elsewhere."

"No, no..." mumbled a goblin girl. "We sleep now." She looked like the leader of the gang. She sprawled audaciously, taking up more space than her kin, and she had constructed a bed out of a pile of books.

Sacrilegious, thought Maribella.

She approached the goblin girl and placed hands on hips. "No, you will *not* sleep now. It's time to get up."

"Five more minutes," said the goblin girl.

"I beg your pardon?"

"You're pardoned." The goblin girl rolled over and began snoring.

"Oh! But you're some annoying little goblins. You there! Goblin girl! I said to *wake up!*"

The goblin girl slowly rolled over, and her closed eyes somehow made contact with Maribella's own, and the eyelids carefully opened just a tiny amount, revealing the yellow irises within. The goblin girl lazily smacked the lips to her wide mouth, swallowed deliberately, and announced:

"One turkey sandwich, please."

And then she rolled back over.

"That goes and does it," said Maribella, and she reached down to grab the goblin.

A mighty snapping and clomping sound echoed through the bookshop, and Maribella recoiled, pulling back her hand the instant before the goblin girl bit down on it. The vicious little creature had oodles of tiny, razor sharp teeth, and Maribella found herself rubbing her hand at the mere thought of getting it caught in that trap.

And just like that, the goblin girl rolled back over and fell immediately to sleep.

"Fine then," said Maribella. "If that's the way you want to play it, then we can do that. I'll go right down to the Town Guard and let the Captain know right away that there are vagrants living on my property. Yes, we'll see how you like that. I'll do things nice and legal and by the book."

Chapter 2

Maribella Hires a Murder-Hobo

Maribella arrived at the Town Guard headquarters to find a jolly-looking fellow sleeping peacefully at his desk. If you just now imagined he was an overweight man, you would be wrong, because he was very skinny, and you should also once more take a good hard look at your prejudices.

"Does everyone in this town simply sleep all day?" Maribella asked herself. The man stirred and thankfully he was far more polite than the pack of goblins back at the Cozy Quill Bookshop.

"Oh," he said. "Hello there young miss. You went and caught me sleeping. Sorry about that, the days can be awfully boring sometimes. If only there was something I could do while sitting for long periods of time." He looked at his empty hands forlornly.

"Actually, I might be able to—"

"So how can I help you?"

"Oh. Yes. Well I'm looking for the Captain of the Town Guard."

"You're in luck, because you just found him. The name is Captain Hargle. Not to be confused with my twin brother, Captain Bargle, the boat captain down by the river."

Maribella exhaled with relief. "Thank the heavens. How do you do, Captain Hargle. My name is Maribella Waters. I've just arrived in town from...well, from abroad, and upon entering my newly purchased property I've found a gang of little squatters squatting inside."

"Squatters!" exclaimed Captain Hargle.

"Yes, squatters. I assume squatting is very much an illegal activity?"

"It is indeed, Ms Waters. Part of the King's decree and all, and included in the town laws as well, it is."

"That's good, then. I was hoping you could assist in delivering an eviction notice to them at once."

"But of course! I'll even wrangle up a few of my men for the express purpose. What was the property?"

"The Cozy Quill Bookshop."

The Captain thought for a moment, then his eyes lit up. "Ah! Yes, that old place. The old woman who used to own it passed away quite a long time ago. Going on twenty years, now? My how time flies." He squinted his eyes and rubbed at his beard, looking off into the distance. "No family or people to bequeath it to, I'd heard. So it defaulted to the Baron's House, and it's been sitting vacant for all these years."

"That's all some very helpful exposition, thank you Captain Hargle."

"So someone finally went and bought it, did they?"

"They did indeed, that someone being me."

"But my, how'd you afford a place like that?"

"I suppose nobody wanted it is all."

The Captain smiled and nodded. "Well all right, then. We'll get you in right shape quick as a rabbit. You can even come along. Tell me, how old are the little cretins?"

"How old are they? Why, I'm not certain."

"All right, then how big are they?"

"About two to three feet tall, I would say."

"Two to three feet tall! But my word, they must be the youngest gang of urchins this town has ever seen. I'll have to tell the Baron we'll need to have a town meeting on the subject of parents looking after their idle children better." The Captain grabbed his sword belt and began buckling it on.

"Children?" said Maribella. "Oh, no, these goblins looked quite full grown."

Captain Hargle froze, his back turned to Maribella. Slowly, his head swiveled about. "What was that you just said?"

"I said these goblins looked quite full grown. I don't believe they're children."

The Captain sighed and his shoulders slumped. He unbuckled his sword belt and placed it back on its hook. "They're goblins, you say?"

"Yes. I don't understand. Why should that matter?"

"Now look here, missy. The kingdom of Plie Brulee is a goodhearted one. A good and honest one, with a good and honest king. And the town of Leafhaven is no different, and Baron Blauca is a stickler for the rules and he follows the rules of his king. We don't go around breaking those rules in this town, now."

"Rules?" said Maribella. "What rules?"

The Captain huffed and strode over to the wall, where a painted poster had been nailed. It depicted a dead goblin (with little X's as eyes) with a sword plunged into its body. A big X had been crossed through the entire picture. Above the picture, it read:

Do Your Part!

Below the picture it read:

Stop Killing Goblins!

"I don't understand," said Maribella.

"Goblins are an endangered species," said Captain Hargle. "You're not from around here, are you, Ms Waters?"

"Oh, no, like I said, I'm from...away. I had no idea. They're truly an endangered species?"

"Truly."

"But I thought there were always so many of them."

"There used to be, at one point in time. But then too many

heroes went on quests. They make for good experience, after all. Fighting experience. You know how it is. These heroic types like to go around battling beasties of the wild. Your kobolds, your blue slimes, your pixies, your imps. Goblins are right there along with them all. And now there are hardly any left. So the King announced a decree for all of Plie Brulee, Leafhaven included. No goblin is to be killed or harmed. Or even touched! Wherever a goblin lay, you are to leave them there and not touch them. And I mean honestly, the whole town loves a good goblin. Who doesn't?"

"Are...are you serious?"

"I'm Hargle."

"You're telling me I have to live with a gang of lazy goblins inside my bookshop?"

"I am. Unless they move of their own accord."

"How am I supposed to run a store with a goblin infestation?"

The Captain mightily shrugged. "Hargle don't make the rules, Hargle just enforces 'em."

"Hmph. Well this is entirely disappointing. Is there truly nothing else I can do?"

And at this point, Captain Hargle stooped his head down and looked over his left shoulder, and then over his right shoulder, and then his left again just for good measure, and when he spoke his voice was a whisper. "Aye. Now, you didn't hear this from me."

"Of course not," whispered Maribella, drawing closer.

"Now see, roughing up goblins would be considered illegal and underhanded work, as we've previously established."

"Well established."

"So someone with a standing like my own couldn't possibly get involved in that kind of work."

"Out of the question."

"But, what a less respectful man would tell you is to go and hire someone less reputable to do your dirty work."

"Ah, yes, I see. And who exactly would this person be?"

"Why, a murder-hobo, of course."

"A *what?*"

The two of them relaxed their postures and stood normally now, and their voices were no longer whispers.

"Surely you've heard of murder-hobos," said the Captain.

"I most certainly have not heard of murder-hobos, and I'm not certain I'm not entirely offended by the term. What in heaven's name is a murder-hobo?"

"Well, perhaps you know them better as adventurers? Swords-for-hire? Mercenaries? Sellswords? You see, a murder-hobo is a man or woman who travels all about the land. They have no home. Their primary source of income is doing odd jobs for the people they come across. Now these jobs could be anything, and any number of solutions could be used to address these jobs, but to a murder-hobo, murdering is usually the go-to strategy. They carry large swords and are excellent fighters. So that's why people call them murder-hobos."

"That's awful. They sound like terrible people. Where could I find them?"

"You'll want to head to the local dark and seedy tavern in town, the Bloody Stump."

"My word. What a horrible name that is. I hope I should never step foot in a place with such a terrible name. Where would I find this tavern?"

"All the way down Main Street to the southern end of town, then turn left and go through some dark alleys by the river docks. At the end of one of them is the Bloody Stump. You can ask around if you get lost, but avoid anyone who's sharpening a knife. There you'll find plenty of brave adventurers, and one of them I'm sure would be happy to help you with your goblin problem."

"Thank you, good Captain. I'm in your debt."

"Don't mention it." He smiled and stuck his thumbs in his belt, then got serious. "I mean it, don't mention this to any townspeople. I could lose my job."

"Of course. And for those very same townspeople's

benefit, I would never go and visit a tavern like the Bloody Stump."

Chapter 3

Maribella Visits the Bloody Stump

It was a chill autumn day, and it felt like the first blustery wind of the season was rolling in. Leaves fluttered and flew off their branches, and Maribella wrapped her arms around herself.

She had made it to the southern end of town and saw a few alleys that looked good and dank, but wasn't certain which dank alley the Bloody Stump resided in. Luckily she once again came across the boy with the hoop and stick.

"Tra la la!" he sang.

"Oh, a familiar face," said Maribella. "You there, do you happen to know where the Bloody Stump is? It's a tavern."

"Of course I do," said the boy. "But first, I've a joke!"

"I didn't ask for one, but let's hear it."

"There was a man building a house with bricks below a high bridge. By the end, he had one brick left over. Have you any idea what he did with the last brick?"

"I don't."

"He threw it straight up into the air. Tra la la!"

And then the boy ran off with his hoop and stick, leaving Maribella standing there frowning at him. "That's not a joke!" she shouted and shook her fist. "Jokes have punchlines! There was no punchline there!" She angrily exhaled and turned back to the alleys. "My word, what an incredibly unhelpful and filthy child."

Maribella relied on blind luck and picked an alley. It twisted about this way and that, and she was about to turn back when she came upon a signpost that said:

Bloody Stump
Cloak Required

There was an arrow pointing in the correct direction, and finally Maribella arrived.

She was relieved that even the seediest tavern in Leafhaven still had some decorative pumpkins sitting out front. It was a pumpkin town, after all. These pumpkins, however, were all poorly formed and some of them were rotten. Very shady pumpkins, you might say, with questionable pasts. The kind of pumpkins you didn't want to be around, especially late at night.

Maribella stepped inside the building to smell smoke and a slight moisture in the air. It was dark. Flickering candles failed to provide much light to do anything, really, and Maribella wondered how the place stayed in business.

"Halt there," came a deep voice. The doorman held out his hand and glared down at Maribella with complete disapproval. He was a rough-looking character, almost as rough as those pumpkins sitting out front, with big shoulders and arms. "There's no way I'm letting you in here, lass..."

"What?" said Maribella. "Why ever not? Is my coin not good?"

"...no indeed, there's no way I'm letting the likes of *you* step one foot in this tavern..." He frowned at her, squinting his eyes and clenching his fists. "...not without a cloak, that is." His posture relaxed and he crossed his arms, nodding his head. After he relaxed, Maribella realized that he was actually a very young man, couldn't have been much past eighteen, with a bit of a dopey look about him and shaggy blond hair.

"A cloak?" asked Maribella.

"Them's the dress code."

"But I don't have a cloak with me."

"No problem, miss. Here you go."

He pointed to a big box with a sign over it that read:

Complimentary Mysterious Cloaks

"Oh. Well that's convenient," said Maribella.

"Here you are," said the doorman, reaching in and pulling out one of the smaller cloaks. He helped wrap it around Maribella's shoulders and pinned the front.

"Thank you," said Maribella, and she started to walk into the common room.

"Ah, not so fast," said the doorman.

"What is it now?"

The doorman grabbed the hood of her cloak and flipped it up so it hid most of her face. "There we are," he said with an approving smile. "Nice and mysterious. Off you go, now."

Maribella finally entered the interior of the Bloody Stump, and thankfully there were no actual bloody stumps to be found. There were plenty of ne'er-do-wells, however, along with a good mix of shady people, and even some shifty ones. All of them wore hooded cloaks. She spotted a bar with a barkeep cleaning mugs with what looked like a dirty rag, and so she decided to head in that direction.

As she passed by table after table, what was it that she heard whispered among patrons? Go on, you know the answer. Why *rumors*, of course.

"Rumor is," whispered one hairy man to his hairy friend (who both wore hooded cloaks), "the Lady Malicent is looking to expand her properties in town."

His friend nodded sagely, and whispered back. "Rumor is, she's got Baron Blauca under her thumb, and he'll do whatever she asks."

Hmm, local politics, thought Maribella. She continued moving on through the room.

"Rumor is," said a hard-looking woman with an eyepatch,

"the Ha-Mazan Tribes have started invading the border lands to Fraey Tarta."

Her friend shook his head. "Looks like Fraey Tarta won't be a kingdom no more, tiny as it already is."

Maribella's mood soured.

And as she drifted closer to the bar, the next rumors did nothing to help.

"Rumor is, the King of Fraey Tarta is enlisting all the young men there to fight back against the Tribes."

"Rumor is, the Queen of Fraey Tarta has taken deathly ill, and she's confined to her bedchambers at all times."

Maribella squeezed her fists and finally made it to the bar. The barkeep squinted one eye at her, not stopping from cleaning his mugs. Maribella's fears were confirmed—the rag was indeed quite dirty.

"Will it be whiskey or ale?" he grunted, his voice like a lizard who'd spent too much time in the sun.

"Neither, thank you," said Maribella. "I'm looking for some help, actually, and I was wondering if you'd point me in the right direction."

"And what kind of help you be lookin' for? Whose throat needs cuttin'?"

Maribella's eyes went wide. "My *word*. I most definitely do *not* need any throats cut. I simply need the help of...well..." She looked around. "An adventurer?"

"A what?"

"You know. An...adventurer? As in, a traveling adventurer?"

"I don't follow."

"A heroic adventurer who helps people for coin?"

"Come again?"

"A sellsword?"

"What's this now?"

"A mercenary soldier of fortune?"

"You'll have to elaborate."

"A sword-for-hire? One that travels from place to place

and doesn't have a home?"

"I have no idea what you're talking about."

Maribella sighed. "A murder-hobo."

"Ah, why didn't you say so?" The barkeep turned to the common room and roared, his voice silencing all conversation. "Oy! Lads! Does the Bloody Stump have any murder-hobos?"

"*Aye!*" came a chorus of rowdy shouts. Men laughed and tankards clashed together, and buckets of ale were completely wasted as drinks spilled to the floor.

Maribella felt her face go red. *This is starting to get out of hand*, she thought, drawing her hood down further.

"Well then?" said the barkeep. "Go on, lass. Tell them the job, see if you get any takers."

Maribella stepped forward, feeling all eyes on her. "Well...I...I suppose I'd like to evict some squatters who are living in my property."

The crowd murmured, nudging each other and nodding their heads. Things looked promising.

"Only, I must clarify, the squatters are goblins."

The murmurs turned to grumbles, and the crowd turned away from Maribella and back to their tables and drinks and card games and rumors.

"Sorry lass," said the barkeep. "Goblins be protected by the laws of Plie Brulee, they be. Even these cutthroats won't be wanting to go against the King's decree on that."

"Yes, I see."

Oh, how depressing a fresh defeat is! How is one to get over it? Time heals all wounds, they say, but Maribella figured she'd be wounded for a long time. That was it. Nobody could help her remove the goblins. Which meant they would stay at her bookshop forever. Which meant she'd have to advertise on theme if she wanted to be a success. "Come for the goblins! Stay for the books!" That sort of thing.

But then, a life-saving rope was flung into the storming ocean waters.

"Girl," said a voice that was both rough and deep yet

distinctly feminine.

Maribella stopped and turned. In the darkest corner of the Bloody Stump, where hardly any candlelight reached, behind a small table sat a woman who was anything but small. It was hard to judge just how large she was while she was sitting down and engulfed in darkness, but from what Maribella could tell, she was a giant.

"Yes?" said Maribella.

"I will handle your goblin problem." The woman spoke with a distinct accent, thick and plodding.

"What about the laws saying goblins aren't to be disturbed?"

"I am not from this kingdom. I am traveler, so I care not for these laws concerning little goblin creatures."

Maribella squinted her eyes. "I'm *pretty* certain that's not how laws work. I think you might still—"

"Goblins are weak and small things. Lazy and lacking in much training, with terrible manners. Like butter-eating fat boy-child who sleeps in late, yes? I will handle these goblins for you. For the right price."

"Oh, I certainly have money. I'll pay you well. I simply need the goblins out of my property."

"I will do this job, then. Come now. Lead me to your house of goblins."

"Oh." Maribella started and stopped, feeling a bit awkward. She had never hired a murder-hobo before, and wasn't sure about all the rules. "My name is Maribella Waters, by the way. It's a pleasure to meet you. May I know your name?"

And here, the woman stood and emerged from the shadows.

She was indeed a giant. Had to have been seven feet tall, and with matching muscles to boot. Despite wearing civilized leather trousers and a clean tunic, the woman was the most barbaric person Maribella had ever seen. A massive battle axe was strung at her back, and her arms were decorated with either paint, or worse yet, tattooed designs of brutish nature. Her skin was golden from days under the sun, and marked with one battle scar after another, including but not limited to slashing scars, stabbing scars, arrowhead scars, and bite scars.

She wore a hooded cloak of course (Maribella was fairly certain it was another Complimentary Mysterious Cloak), and when she flipped the hood back and revealed her face, Maribella put fingers to her mouth and gasped inward.

The sides of the giant's head were shaved close. The hair on top sprang upward as if it were alive, and it stood straight up a good foot at least, making the woman look even taller. It resembled the head plumage of a furious egret desperately looking for a mate. Piercings ran the length of her ears, along with a few on her nose, and either black warpaint or more tattoo work adorned the area around her blue eyes, making them stand out fiercely in contrast.

The wooden boards creaked heavily under her weight as she stepped forward and placed clenched fists on her hips, the muscles on her shoulder and biceps bulging quite impressively as far as muscles go.

"I am Asteria Helsdottir, of the Ha-Mazan Tribes."

Maribella's skin went cold, and her breath caught in her lungs.

She had just hired a member of the people currently attacking the kingdom of Fraey Tarta.

Chapter 4

Asteria Goes to Work

As Maribella and Asteria walked out the Bloody Stump, they passed the doorman who sighed heavily and said, "Oh, but if only there was something I could do while sitting here for hours on end." He stared at his empty hands wistfully, as if wishing something could fill them.

Maribella wasn't in best form, though, so she just walked on by, side by side with the barbarian from the north.

A Ha-Mazan warrior, in the flesh, walking right next to her, in her employ. It was as if fate itself had intervened. Maribella fought every urge to panic and run the opposite direction as fast as her feet could take her.

She glanced sideways at Asteria. The stories they told of the Ha-Mazan Tribes were apparently true. The men grew as big as any other men, but the women were all giants, and hence in charge, naturally.

"What is the woman-child looking at?" asked Asteria.

"Excuse me?" said Maribella. "Are you referring to me?"

"Who else would I be speaking to?"

"I'm not a woman-child. I'm twenty-three years old, if you must know."

"All southern women are women-children. Small and breakable."

"Well that's rather rude."

"It is fact of life."

"Well in that case, if you must know, I was looking at *you*. Because you're so giant and strange, unlike all other southern women, who are perfectly acceptable sizes."

Asteria actually smiled. It was a small one, but it counted. "When in the den of wolves, one must walk on all fours and lap at water."

"Come again?"

"I concede. Here in land of Plie Brulee, I am indeed strange."

Eventually they reached the Cozy Quill Bookshop, and they stood quietly just looking at the building for half a minute.

"What is this place?" asked Asteria.

"It's a bookshop. I just bought it. I'm new in town, you see. I purchased the deed and did all business via mail with the Baron, and this is the place where the goblins have moved in."

"Book...shop?"

"Yes?"

"What is...book...shop?"

"It's a shop where you buy books."

Asteria turned her head and looked down at Maribella. Maribella suddenly felt very small.

"An entire building? That only sells books? Such a thing exists?"

"Well of course it does."

Asteria looked back up to the Cozy Quill. "Falling stars, I've never heard of such a thing."

"You don't have books in Ha-Mazan?"

"We do, but they are rare and valuable. Guarded. They are not just sold in store like animal skins."

Maribella cleared her throat. "Well, these books won't be sold either, not unless something is done about those goblins."

Asteria grew serious. "Yes. I will now proceed to slaughter goblins. Prepare for much spilling of blood." She reached around and removed the enormous battle axe from her back and gripped it tightly.

"Wait, what?"

"I will now kill goblins. Wait outside. Unless you would like to watch. I will not judge."

"No, you will *not* kill goblins." Maribella dashed about and stood in front of Asteria, which was only slightly harrowing. She placed her hands on her hips and glared up at the giantess. "There is to be no goblin-killing today, thank you very much."

"I am much confused now. You hired me to handle problem of goblins, yes?"

"I did. But I didn't intend for you to kill them."

"Then what did you intend for me to do? Ask them nicely to leave?"

"Well, no, not exactly that either. Hmm, let me think."

And she did so. She turned about, looking from the Cozy Quill's front door to the Ha-Mazan warrior and back. She place a few fingers on her lips, and she hummed.

"How about you go inside, but leave your axe out here? And you can just throw them out."

"Throw them?"

"Yes, toss them. They look to be about the same size and weight as a sack of potatoes, after all. You can kick them a little, too, but not hard enough to really hurt them. Just watch out for your fingers. They can be a bit bitey, especially the girl goblin. She's their leader, you see."

"Hmm." Asteria looked from her battle axe, which she clearly adored, to the Cozy Quill. She shrugged. "Such is life. I lap at the puddles of wolves."

"The wha—"

"Hold this." She let the axe fall toward Maribella, who almost fell over in her effort to catch and hold it. She watched as Asteria entered the bookshop and a good minute went by.

Perhaps I should have prepared her for the sheer number of books inside, she thought. *She seemed awed by the mere mention of books. Dozens upon dozens of them on shelves may have overwhelmed her.*

After another minute, the front door burst open and banged against the wall. A goblin came running out with his arms in the air, letting out a shrill shout. He ran in a serpentine pattern across the road, avoiding Maribella, and disappeared into a side street.

A second goblin stumbled out the building, just as terrified as the first, and then a third. They both ran in separate directions. A great clattering rang out from inside the shop, and Maribella worried that a battle might be damaging the building, or even worse, the books.

The goblins began to stream out from the bookshop like rats leaving a sinking ship. They flung themselves out windows, tripped over themselves getting through the door, and one even crawled his way out from a small hole near the ground at the side of the building.

There was no goblin girl to be found, though.

The goblins had all disappeared, and there was finally silence. Then came the footsteps. Heavy, plodding, angry footsteps.

Asteria emerged, and she carried the goblin girl. One hand gripped the back of the neck of her shirt, while another hand gripped the back of her belt. All four goblin limbs hung limply, as if the goblin girl was employing a form of non-violent resistance.

Asteria presented the creature to Maribella. The goblin girl lifted her head, black hair framing her face, and her eyelids were still heavy with sleep.

"Is this leader?" asked Asteria.

"That's the one," said Maribella. "She tried to bite me."

"I was hungry," said the goblin girl with a shrug.

"I will now proceed to throw her," said Asteria.

"I have a name, you know," said the goblin girl, surprising both women. "It's Gidget. Gidget the Goblin Girl."

"Well how do you do, Gidget the Goblin Girl?" said Maribella. "Now good day, and may we never meet again."

It was at this point that something very strange happened. That's not to say the day wasn't strange before this moment; it was exceptionally strange. But this next bit was strange even compared to the rest of the day.

Gidget let the most mystifying smile come over her face. It was smug and self-satisfied. Close-lipped and heavy-lidded. Like the face of a cat who just ate a bird and was quite pleased about how everything turned out.

"I'll be around if you need me, kid," she said to Maribella, never losing her smile.

And then Asteria tossed her into the air after spinning about once to build up some momentum. It was like watching a legendary athlete break a record. Gidget the Goblin Girl went flying down the street, and landed squarely into a large wagon filled with hay.

"That was an amazing throw!" cried Maribella, clapping her hands together.

"Thank you," said Asteria. "I have much experience throwing goblins."

"Here you are." Maribella handed the axe back, eager to be rid of it. "Well then, that's that. Money owed for a job well done. Here you are." She handed over a few coins.

"This is good. But what about my retainer?"

"Your retainer?"

"Yes. I will be needing salary now."

"I don't understand. Salary for what?"

"For my continued service as bookshop guard. I can also lift heavy objects and reach high places. I am much useful, you will find."

"Oh, I believe there's been a mistake. I only needed you for the one job. We can go our separate ways now."

"A shop with that many books will need a guardian. A protector."

Maribella couldn't help but laugh a little, but she caught herself and tried to stay serious. "Oh, I don't think Leafhaven is really all that dangerous a place. Other than those goblins, I don't think I'll be having any more problems."

"You never know. And besides, the goblins will quickly come back if I leave."

"I wouldn't bet on *that*. You outright terrified them. Why I'm sure they're leaving town at this very moment. No, you can go back to the Bloody Stump with the other murder-hobos, Ms Helsdottir. I don't think I'll be seeing those goblins again anytime soon."

Chapter 5

Goblins Once Again Squat at the Cozy Quill

T he goblins immediately came back. It was later that day, in fact. Maribella ran down to the Bloody Stump and hired Asteria again, and everything pretty much played out exactly how it played out the first time, complete with Gidget the Goblin Girl getting thrown into the wagon of hay, so we won't go over any of that a second time.

But this time Maribella agreed to keep Asteria on as the first official employee of the Cozy Quill Bookshop.

Chapter 6

Maribella and Asteria Explore the Bookshop

Maribella ran her hand along the rows of books in amazement. It was more than she could hope for. Volumes upon volumes of every kind of book she could think of, from nonfiction such as histories and biographies and texts on all manner of practical occupations, to fiction that included all the most famous publications of the last several decades. Aside from some spiderwebs that needed dusting, and dust that also needed dusting, they were in great condition.

"I almost want to just sit and read them all right now," she said.

"Hmm," hummed Asteria, looking solemn. She stood in the center of the bookshop and looked about, as if afraid of getting too close to the shelves. "You probably should. If you sell them, you will not have any books."

"That's why I'll be buying more."

"More?"

"That's right. I buy them, then sell them. That's how it works."

"There are truly that many books?"

"Truly. Have you read any yourself?"

Asteria frowned. "Hmm. No."

"Why not? It's a lovely hobby to have in my opinion."

"I mean that I do not know *how* to read. Or at least, not

very well. I am very slow at the reading, and the words all mash together."

"Oh, I see." Maribella's first instinct was the shake Asteria by the shirt and yell at her that she needed to improve her reading skills as soon as possible, but she didn't think that would go over too well with the seven foot tall, axe-toting, bloodthirsty barbarian. Instead, she said, "Well, I'll have to teach you to read better one of these days. But for now, we need to explore this building and clean it up. I hope to open quickly."

They spent the day first exploring the place. Maribella soon realized that it was far more elaborate a building than it first seemed. There was more than one simple main first floor area. There were many nooks and crannies, little corners and hideaways. Some of them were places to simply sit and read in by a warm brazier, and some of them had their own tiny little bookshelf with a small collection of books.

"So many books," said Asteria. "How is this possible? This building must have immeasurable fortune within."

"Maybe many years ago you would be right, back when we had to copy books by hand," said Maribella. "But these days, most books are made by printing press."

"Printing...press?"

"Yes. An ingenious inventor named Joan Flugenflurgen came up with the idea. It's a machine that can press ink to page all at once, thereby making copies of books much faster than the old way. That's how this many books can be so affordable, you see. But I'm sure there are a few expensive hand-written ones hidden away. We'll need to do a thorough search."

"Still though, how were you able to afford such great purchase? Building and books together?"

"I suppose nobody wanted it and I just got lucky."

"Hmm. Such a mysterious shop of books. You said before it has been closed for many years, yes?"

"That's right."

"Why did no thieves enter to rob it, then? Except for sleeping goblins, it looks like nobody has been here."

Maribella looked at Asteria as if she were a mad woman. "Because the store has been closed all this time, of course, so it wouldn't be polite to steal from it. Really Asteria, use your head."

While poking about the shop, Maribella wanted to do everything at once right away, but she found that she had to be methodical. With the day getting colder, she needed to start a few of the fireplaces in the room.

"We need wood, I suppose," she said, rubbing at her own arms.

"There is woodcutter down the road. You may buy wood there."

"Come with me?"

At the woodcutter's shop they also realized they needed a cart, so Maribella bought that as well, and Asteria hauled the pile of wood along with some other supplies back to the shop. While Asteria unloaded the bulk of it behind the shop, Maribella struggled at the main hearth of the shop, which resided in the center back of the main first floor room. Two comfortable chairs faced it, along with a little table.

"Uh," she said intelligently, holding two blocks of wood in her hands. She placed them randomly in the fireplace, and then placed small twigs on top. The best thing to do with the flint at the time was simply hold it in her hands, she figured.

Asteria came back and stared at her, arching an eyebrow that had no right being as expressive as it was. "Why is fire not lit?"

"Uh, here you go." Maribella handed her the flint.

Asteria looked at the wood and shook her head. "This is not the way to build fire. Have you never built fire before?"

"Of course I have. We just...do it differently where I'm from."

"And where is that?"

"From abroad, of course."

"Here." Asteria knelt and arranged the wood the proper way, then lit it by striking iron against flint. The atmosphere of the room almost immediately improved, changing from dark and dreary and cold to warm and colorful.

Asteria warmed her hands near the flames, and Maribella joined her. Together they listened to the wood catch and crackle in the quiet.

"I will teach you to make fire," said Asteria. Maribella didn't respond, and they knelt in silence for a while.

"All right then," said Maribella. "Time to keep exploring."

"We will need candles in the dark."

"Candles! Oh, I think not! A fire in the fireplace is all well and good, but there is to be no candles or any other open flame carried about in this building. These books are all highly flammable, of course."

"Then how will we see?"

"Watch this."

She arranged two glass containers with handles on them that she had brought with her on her travels, and placed some flowers and leaves within them. "Glowbug flowers," she explained.

"I do not understand."

"We'll leave them here for a few minutes." She placed both glasses on the open windowsill and went back to exploring the shop.

They found doors that led to more books, and some doors were locked. Maribella didn't have any other keys other than the front door key.

"I will now proceed to break down door for you," said Asteria.

"No, no, that will be fine. Not now, at least. We can get into these other rooms later. For now, let's keep going and try not to break anything."

After exploring a bit, they came to what looked like an altar set against a wall, and on this altar was a glass case, and inside this glass case was a very large and very old-looking book.

Maribella gasped, her eyes growing wide, and she almost smashed her face against the glass. "I can't believe it! I can't believe this is here!"

"A podium and glass case with rotten beaver log inside?"

"This isn't a rotten beaver log, it's a book. A very old and expensive book."

"Yes, books are expensive."

"This one more than most. This is an original printing of an Isambard Ruskin novel."

"Ah. Yes. Of course."

"It's called *The Excursion of the One Who Longs to Penetrate the Curtains of the Strange*. It's a massive novel about a man's journey around the world."

"It is very good book, then?"

"Heavens no. Isambard Ruskin was a pioneer in many things, but it'd be impossible to actually enjoy his work today. It's so archaic and long. At many points he'll just go on and on about various landscapes, bugs, clouds and the like, and start philosophizing about nonsensical things. The book has no plot, basically, and is highly famous for being a tedious bore."

"Hmm. Then why is this book so valuable if it is so terrible?"

"Because the value is in the book itself, not the words. This is an original. The thing itself is an artifact for collectors. Oh, I'll have to research the price on this one. Only let it go to the wealthiest of buyers. I might even just keep it here with the bookshop forever, in fact."

After getting over her amazing discovery, she led Asteria back to the jars to find them glowing brightly with green, floating dots. Maribella smiled. "Glowbugs are attracted to the glowbug flowers, of course. Put some in empty glass like this, and you've soon got a natural lantern. See?"

She lifted one by the handle and offered it to Asteria. "Falling stars," she said in awe. The color lit up her face.

"Now we can have light without the risk of burning the place down."

They found a boarded up passageway in the very back of the building. Maribella allowed Asteria to pull the boards off, which revealed a dark and gloomy hallway, short and cramped.

A heavy, dark door was at the end, locked. A sign was hammered onto it that said:

Do Not Enter

"Hmm, how curious," said Maribella. She could have sworn she heard strange sounds, something barely audible, and so she placed her ear against the door.

Sinister whispering came from within the room. She narrowed her eyes, focusing, and made out several words.

"Stay out..."

"Beware..."

"Turn back..."

"Gladly," said Maribella. "Hammer those boards back up, Asteria. There will be no adventures today, thank you very much."

Asteria did just so and they moved on.

Stairs led up to a second floor. The main room of the building had a balcony with yet more books wrapping all around it, and this area led to several other rooms. One of them was a quaint bedroom. Everything was neat and tidy, if a bit dusty. The bed was made, the dressers were empty, and there was even a little table and chair next to the window that looked out behind the bookshop. A portrait hung on the wall of a pretty young woman with curly hair.

"This'll be my room," said Maribella. "Pretty smart, sleeping at your own bookshop, isn't it? It'll save me plenty of money."

"And where will I be sleeping?"

"At your own home, naturally."

"I have no home. I am very transient. Such is life for me now."

"Oh, yes, murder-hobo and all. Well that's a bit sad. I suppose you could stay here then. It would do good to have someone guard the place at night as well. We could get some blankets and pillows and you can sleep wherever you want down on the first floor. You could be like a guard dog."

"This will be done."

They found more locked doors on the second floor, and they had still yet to discover the passage that led up to the tiny tower that sat right on top of the building.

"We'll have to finish exploring later. For now we need to clean things up."

The rest of the day was spent doing just so. They used brooms and the cart to get rid of most of the big debris, and whatever mess the goblins had made was set right. The cobwebs were swept away, the thick layers of dust were dusted. They drew water from the nearby well and washed the windows until they were crystal clear. By the time evening fell, the Cozy Quill Bookshop was finally starting to look cozy.

The two women stood on the balcony, hands on hips, and surveyed their work.

"What a change!" said Maribella. "I do believe that we can open tomorrow morning, first thing."

Asteria looked at her incredulously. "Tomorrow? So soon?"

"Yes. Why not?"

"You have just arrived. You do not even know what all books you have."

"But that's just the thing. Our customers can wander in and find out alongside us. They can browse while we do the very same thing."

"Browse?"

"Yes, browse. Walk about aimlessly, heads tilted and craned, slowly lumbering around while reading titles and authors. It's the best way to shop for a book, honestly. You see something that might look interesting, so you pull it off the shelf, sit in one of those chairs there, and read it a bit. Then you either buy it or you don't."

Asteria looked amazed.

"That's what's so great about my decision to buy this store," continued Maribella. "The product is already all available.

I don't have to build it or cook it. I already own it. We can keep working on the shop while it's open. Just wait and see."

They ate a simple dinner of buttered bread and apples in front of the fireplace together, exhausted from the day's work, and soon retired to their respective beds. As Maribella lay under her blankets, tucked in tight and warm while cold wind howled outside her window, she listened to the building creaking. It felt alive to her, like she was inside the belly of a giant beast.

She suddenly realized that if everything had gone as she originally intended, she would have been very frightened as she lay there in her new room. But thankfully, things didn't go as intended. You might even say she encountered nothing but problem after problem since arriving in town.

And thanks to that, she had a barbarian sleeping just downstairs, and so she didn't feel frightened at all.

She fell asleep quickly, her last drifting thoughts of what a success her new bookshop would be.

Chapter 7

The Bookshop is a Complete Failure

The next morning Maribella found the open sign and placed it on the front door, and then stood outside by the display window for ten minutes. Nobody stopped or entered the shop.

"Hmm," said Maribella after going back inside. "I suppose ten minutes isn't much time for people to notice I'm open. I need to be a bit more patient."

After thirty minutes there were still no customers and that's when Maribella began to get worried. She spent the morning exploring the books to take her mind off customers, and found them to be organized well by subject and then author. Asteria wandered about the building, poking at things that looked like they needed poking. She also looked in nook and crannies, just to make sure there were no goblins hiding about.

"I must say," said Maribella. "I do find myself having the time of my life learning more about this wonderful collection of books, but I'm beginning to worry we won't ever get any customers."

Asteria sagely grunted, her impressive arms crossed.

"I suppose it was a bit silly to just open up and expect people to instantly buy what I'm selling. I need to somehow get the word out."

Asteria grunted in agreement again.

"But I've no knowledge of effective advertising," continued

Maribella. "How do I get the word out? Do you have any ideas, Asteria?"

"Back in my tribe, when something is to be sold, the seller will shout of their wares to passing people. If the passing people ignore the shouting, a challenge may be offered by the merchant if she or he wishes. Combat will be had in street, and the customer must purchase goods if she or he loses. Merchant must slink away in shame, and her or his products are known as inferior goods of little quality for one week following. This is timeless and true method of commerce in Ha-Mazan Tribes."

"Uh," said Maribella. "I don't think I'll be challenging anyone to combat anytime soon. Leafhaven wouldn't really get the finer points of that advertising method. I do need to do something, but what..."

She narrowed her eyes in deep thought and stroked her chin. Asteria copied her exactly, until Maribella suddenly got an idea.

"Ah! Yes! That's it! We need to put up fliers and posters all over town. Why, there's probably even a town message board somewhere. Come on now, help me make up some fliers."

They spent most of the morning filling small sheets of parchment with various kinds of advertisements. "The Cozy Quill Bookshop – Now Open For Business!" was the standard format, with the important bits below in smaller letters, such as address and hours of operation. "Put A Book In Your Hand!" was another try, along with "Cheapest Books In Town!" and "Largest Collection Of Books In Town!" She even drew a few pictures of books around the empty spaces of the fliers, along with a rendition of the Cozy Quill itself, which was quite well-done if you asked her (and that's why you should never rely on the artist's opinion for gauging the quality of his or her own art piece).

Asteria offered her a crudely-drawn flier.

"Um," said Maribella. "We'll put it in the *maybe* pile."

At around noon they closed the shop and raced madly about town hammering the fliers on any space that seemed reasonable. Maribella didn't want to be rude, of course, so she tried to be careful and tactful about where she put the advertisements. They went up only in areas with other signage.

They even found the fabled message board in the center of town in an open space called Peabush Square, and there was quite a bit of activity around it. Old gruff men with big white mustaches hammered up jobs, and young strapping men yanked the very same papers off and followed the old gruff men to employment then and there. Shady looking characters in cloaks slipped up messages, and even shadier looking characters slipped them down.

"There we are," said Maribella, instructing Asteria to hammer their advertisement in a nice open spot. "This is sure to get some attention."

They walked away and watched the board for a minute, just to see. Someone almost immediately came and nailed up their own flier over theirs.

"Well this is disheartening," said Maribella. "No matter how many fliers you put up, it seems as if they just get lost in the mix. How are you ever supposed to stand out when so many people are advertising all at once?"

"You must do something different," said Asteria. "Something that nobody else here is doing. That way you stand out."

"Yes, that's exactly right, Asteria."

"Like challenge passersby to combat."

"Perhaps something less violent. Ah, wait! I have it!"

She almost ran back to the bookshop, and then began filling a satchel with various small books. "These little ones are cheap and easy to buy," she said. "They're just fun little productions, such as collections of poems, or a short story, or little essays. It wouldn't be such a bad thing if I gave a few away, would it?" She filled her satchel and then dashed back into town, a curious Asteria following along.

It is at this point in the story that I must inform you this book is interactive. No, it's too late to run now. I'm afraid to say the stage lamp is already on you, dear reader. You're a part of things now.

You will be randomly quizzed over how closely you were paying attention to events so far, and the first quiz will occur right now.

What was the name of the forlorn doorman to the Bloody Stump?

And don't worry, this is a multiple choice quiz.

Was it:

A) Hargle

B) Bargle

C) Gargle

Now think good and hard over it. Don't answer too fast. And no cheating allowed. There is to be no flipping back to earlier in the book. Are you ready?

The answer is none of the above. It was a trick question. The forlorn doorman to the Bloody Stump was never given a name. The Captain of the Town Guard, however, was given a name, and that was Hargle, and that's who Maribella visited next.

"Well hello there, young miss," said Captain Hargle after he was woken up from his nap. "And oh, I see you've made a friend already." He craned his head up to Asteria, nodding politely to her.

"You will make no sudden movements," said Asteria.

"Very well. What can I do for you two today?"

Maribella stepped forward with almost a hop, and presented one of the small books to the Captain.

"What's this, now?" he asked.

"You said the other day that you wished you had something to do while sitting about on your long shifts here. Well, this is a little book for you."

"Ah, is it now! *Peatry's Paltry Collection of Poems and Pontifications*. Ah, I always did enjoy a good pontification. Why thank you, miss. How much do I owe you for this?"

"It's free. But only if you put this flier up in your office."

She handed him a flier. One of the good ones, not the one with the decapitated goblins. "This is the shop I just reopened, the Cozy Quill. Come by any time for more books, and tell all your friends and family."

"Ah, I see! And now it all comes together, it does. You've solved your little goblin problem, eh?" He smiled and tapped his nose and winked. "I'll be sure to send business your way." And then he took a quick nap.

After that they made for the Bloody Stump to deliver a free book to the young doorman. If you *must* quench your insatiable curiosity, his name was Dave.

"Why thank you," he said, flipping through his book titled *Lusty Ladies and Other Lecherous Tales*. "I always did enjoy fine literature. Now I have something to do all shift."

"That's the idea," said Maribella, and she gave him the same offer she had given Captain Hargle.

Together, Maribella and Asteria went about town visiting other stores and various peoples of note. They gave away all the books in the satchel, and the sun was down by the time they made it back to the bookshop. They were both starving, and so they ate ravenously, and then retired to the first floor fireplace together.

"I'm beat," said Maribella, warming her hands over the fire. When she sat down it dawned on her how busy she'd been the past few days. She hadn't had time to stop and be a person. In fact, in the grandest of all irony, she hadn't even time to actually crack open a book and give it a read, and there she was surrounded by them.

Asteria sat in the other chair, both of them facing the fire. The barbarian was generally quiet, and didn't talk unless Maribella started first. She supposed that was a good thing. Asteria was from the Ha-Mazan Tribes, after all.

And yet, she couldn't help but wonder just what someone like herself was doing down south.

"Why aren't you with your tribe?" asked Maribella, and she tensed up as the words left her mouth, as if she hadn't been the one to ask them.

"Hmm," hummed Asteria.

Time passed by. The fire crackled, the logs popped, and strong winds gusted outside, making the building creak.

"I've never seen a Ha-Mazan warrior out of your lands before," said Maribella.

"This is true," said Asteria. Her voice was soft and low, gentle in the quiet of night. "We do not leave our lands. Only an outcast would leave their tribe."

Maribella watched as Asteria gazed into the fire. "So, does that mean you're an outcast? I must admit, I'm not certain what would make someone an outcast where you're from."

Asteria hummed in response again.

"It's just..." said Maribella, her voice falling even quieter, "...I would have thought that you would be with the rest of your people, invading the border of Fraey Tarta. Those are the rumors, that is. That you're invading."

"Yes..." said Asteria, and her stare looked as if it was miles and miles away. "The Queen has decided to invade."

"So I thought...well, I always thought that all Ha-Mazan people loved fighting, loved battle, and with the invasion, well..."

"Some of us do, yes. Some of us grow things. Some of us build things. Some of us battle."

"Yes, of—"

"My family line battles. My family line are the greatest of battlers."

Maribella went silent for a long while, and she couldn't pry her eyes from the giantess. "So..." she said.

Finally, Asteria turned her head to Maribella. "So you are my employer, and I am your employee, and these are questions you do not ask."

Maribella swallowed deeply and went red in the face. After that, she said nothing, and neither did Asteria, and the two sat and watched the fire until sleep made them get up and go to bed.

Chapter 8

Maribella Finds Some Haunted Books

"I don't understand," said Maribella, standing outside the Cozy Quill and looking up and down the street. "There should be customers today. The signs! The free samples!"

"Hmm," said Asteria.

"Why isn't anyone coming in? Morning's almost over." She pulled her coat tighter as a cold wind blew red and yellow leaves down the street. "The leaves are starting to fall. We're knee-deep in Autumn now. The town should be breaking down my door clamoring for books. I mean good heavens, what if it snows? Then where will they be? Without a good book, that's where!"

"Hmm."

"Well." Maribella spent another full minute looking up and down the street. "Guess we better go in."

They went inside and Maribella perused the shelves, this time actually looking for something to read herself. Her tastes were great and varied, but at the moment she figured she might read up on shop-keeping or advertising or economics or the like, if she could find a book on the subjects.

But as she aimlessly wandered down the shelves, she once again came across the boarded up passageway with the locked door behind it. She stopped and heard the whispers even from out on the main floor.

"I suppose we might as well deal with this while we have

the time," she said.

I feel that it would go against my conscience if I didn't now give a warning for what is about to happen. The story is about to get frightening. In fact, it's about to get downright chilling. Maribella is going to open that door, you see. Yes, the very same door where all those creepy whispers are emanating from. You knew it had to be done sooner or later. And so here we are. I'm not exaggerating, things are going to get terrifying once we get past that door and go into the room beyond. Those readers who frighten easily may want to skip ahead a page or two, or at least read the next part while sitting close to someone else you can trust. In fact, I'll even make it easy for you. I'll put big, large, bold headers where the terrifying part begins and ends, that way if you don't want to be terrified then you know where to skip to.

Beginning of Terrifying Section

"There we are," said Maribella as Asteria ripped off the last of the boards, revealing the small, dark passage. Maribella lifted her glowbug lantern and peered inside at the locked door. The whispering came louder from behind that dark wood.

"Are you sure you want to do this thing?" asked Asteria. "It sounds like great evil is inside this room."

"Better to face it now than live with it right next to us all this time, isn't it? All right then, Asteria. Time to give those muscles a workout. I don't have a key for this door, so you're going to have to chop it up with your axe. Are you able to—"

Maribella flinched as Asteria already began to lay into the door. She sent the head of her axe cracking into the wood, splintering pieces with each loud thud. Asteria grunted with every swing, her oversized muscles flexing and twitching about.

I must admit, thought Maribella. *This is quite impressive.*

With one big crash, the door broke right open. Asteria stepped to the side, and Maribella strode in, lifting her glowing lamp.

The room was small and it contained a decent collection

of books for its size. They were large and dark and bound with thick black or red leather. Their fronts were engraved with skulls and faces and stag horns and all manner of evil-looking things. And as Maribella slowly moved through the room, they whispered to her.

"Beware…"

"Evil…"

"Turn back…"

"Cursed books…"

"Do not open us…"

Maribella put her hand to her mouth. "My word," she whispered, her head swiveling all about. "This bookshop even has a cursed section, and we're standing in it."

"Cursed ye be too…"

"Open and be haunted…"

"Heed our warning and turn back…"

"Danger…"

"Beware…"

"By all means," said Maribella, "that sounds like wonderful advice. Into the rubbish you go."

She grabbed a book off the shelf and chunked it right into the cart Asteria had pushed in. She went for another book.

"Wait—" came the mysterious voice from one book as she grabbed it and tossed it in the cart. None of the books whispered now, but spoke in loud and clear voices.

"But we didn't mean—" said the next book.

"Can't we talk about this f—" cried the next one.

"Hey what's the big i—" shouted another.

"Come along, Asteria," said Maribella. "Toss them all into the rubbish. There we go, just like that. Don't open or read them. Right off the shelf and into the trash."

The next several minutes consisted of Maribella and Asteria tossing complaining books into the cart. Once the shelves were empty and the cart was full, Asteria pushed the books out the room, through the bookshop and out the front door. On the side of the street was a little area where some previous townspeople had built up a fire before, and this is where Maribella and Asteria went.

The wind blew cold and chilly, and Maribella rubbed her hands together and blew on them to keep warm. "It's a cold Autumn this year," she said. "Let's start a nice fire."

And so the two women placed a few books within a circle of sooty rocks and Asteria lit them. After stoking the flames a bit, they then began tossing in the cursed books, one right after the other.

The books were still complaining just before being thrown into the flames, although their voices cut off once they hit the fire.

"What's this now? What are you—gah!"

"I think we got off on the wrong—hurk!"

"Don't be so hasty now, we can—wait, no!"

"It has been an honor spending this time with you all," said the last book, which took its burning with honor and dignity.

Soon, the entire cart was empty, and the books were now a raging fire.

End of Terrifying Section

Maribella and Asteria warmed their cold hands over a cheery fire on the edge of the street near the Cozy Quill. "What a delightful day it was today," said Maribella.

"I do miss the cold of the north," agreed Asteria. "It is nice to feel the seasons getting colder down here. Almost reminds me of home."

But as cold as the day was, the fire kept them warm. They looked so pleased with themselves that a few townspeople came over and joined them at the fire.

"The days are getting colder, aren't they?" asked one grateful fellow. "This fire was a lovely idea."

"I agree," said a woman wearing a big, furry coat. "Been a while since we had a nice fire like this. I don't recognize the two of you. Are you new in town?"

"We are, yes," said Maribella. "My name is Maribella and this is my friend Asteria. I just bought and opened up the bookshop here."

"Ah! So you're the new owner of the Cozy Quill, yes? It's been closed forever it seems. I had no idea it was open."

"Well it is now."

"How'd you ever manage to afford a place like this?"

"I don't know, I suppose I just got lucky with the price."

A couple more townspeople gathered around the fire, joining the hand-warming.

"Did you hear?" said the first townswoman. "This here is Maribella, and she's the one who went and bought the Cozy Quill. She's sponsoring this bonfire, she is."

"Oh, is that so?" said an old man. "I used to browse there a long time ago. But my, it's been an age." He walked on two canes and seemed ancient. The top of his head was bald but two tufts of white hair at the sides stuck straight up. Maribella was delighted at the sudden realization that this arrangement of hair was the exact opposite of Asteria's, which was bald on the sides and stuck straight up on top.

"The name is Clarence," he said after receiving a how-do-you-do from Maribella.

"Clarence here owns a flower shop just a few buildings down," explained one of the townspeople. "He's also the oldest living man in town."

"Well that certainly beats being the oldest dead man in town," said Maribella.

"That it does," said Clarence. "But my, what a sight this bookshop is. I was there when it first opened, you know."

"Is that so? May I ask who was the original owner? I purchased it sight unseen from the Baron. I know nothing of the previous owners."

"It's only ever had one. A young woman who grew to be an old woman, she was, who everyone in town adored very much. Yes, a very fine bookshop it was. What a sight it is, seeing it open again..."

Yet more people joined the fire, and the first fellow lifted a finger and walked off excitedly. "Hold on tight, I've an idea. I've got some sausages that need cooking and then eating. Let me go and get them."

So it was that a dozen townspeople cooked sausages on sticks over the fire and ate them. Someone brought out a jug of wine for those who wished for a drink, and a jug of milk for those who didn't drink, and delightful conversation was had all around. Someone was eating the insides of a pumpkin right out of the gourd, and it was quite possible that fellow was also out of his gourd.

"Join the Cozy Quill Bookshop bonfire!" cried a random townsperson, and the size of the group doubled.

Maribella stood in shock. She looked up to Asteria, who shrugged, and then back to the growing crowd.

"Well then," said Clarence the oldest man in town. "Might as well have a trip down memory lane and browse the ol' shop again. Come with me, young lass. I've fours legs to me now, but I don't trust a one of them."

He was the first person to enter the front door to the Cozy Quill, and after him were many more.

The fire eventually died down, but the traffic didn't. People talked and chatted, they browsed and read, they purchased and left and spread the word. Dave the forlorn doorman and Captain Hargle both showed up to buy some books after they had exhausted their free samples.

"Don't think I forgot about you," said Hargle, wagging his finger. "I went and told the friends and family, too."

And so it was for the next several days, business boomed, coins filled the coffers, and Maribella couldn't seem to stop smiling. A whole week went by, and customers told their friends, who told their friends, and so on and so forth. Soon, the Cozy Quill Bookshop was the talk of the town, and it seemed as if everyone wanted to see what the fuss was about and spend at least a few minutes browsing aimlessly down the shelves and aisles, poking about in the little side rooms with their own little libraries, and having a sit in front of the fire to sample a book and perhaps purchase it, or perhaps save the rest for a later free read, as some industrious folks are known to do.

"It's happening, Asteria," said Maribella one day while looking over the small crowd in the shop. "The people finally know we're in business. It's actually going to work out."

Asteria didn't say anything, but she looked down at Maribella, and the smallest of smiles formed on her lips.

For the first time in a long time, Maribella was happy, and there was nothing that would ruin that.

Chapter 9

Lady Malicent Ruins Everything

Every story needs its villain, and the villain of this one is quite vicious. Small children shouldn't be told about her. In fact, there's a good possibility that Lady Malicent eats small children. If you've ever heard a story about an evil witch who tricks children into crawling into an oven so she can cook and consume them with a side of spinach and squash, it was probably Lady Malicent who started the legend. I'm fairly certain she even had her own spinach garden at this point in time. What sort of monster goes and does a thing like that? Who eats spinach voluntarily?

It was a dreary day when she arrived at the Cozy Quill. Dark clouds thundered overhead, but they hadn't decided to rain yet. Townspeople ran in the streets, holding onto their hats and struggling to keep their cloaks closed tightly against the wind, while waves of red and yellow maple leaves blew over them. The scene was all rather foreboding.

She entered the shop as if she owned the place, and sent the bell over the door clattering violently. Behind her was a massive, muscled man who had muscles growing over his muscles. He didn't look like the kind of fellow who solved math equations for a living. In fact, his clenched knuckles were gnarled with calluses as if he spent his free time punching rocks. He glanced about the place like a man searching for his runaway dog.

But Lady Malicent was what drew the eye. She was the queen of icicles everywhere made flesh. Were she to look at you (and believe me, you would not want to be the recipient of her gaze), you would suddenly feel as if you were a tiny insect about to get crushed. She was tall and lean, with a severe and hard face. She had black hair and pale skin stark against a pure black dress that seemed to be designed to appease the tastes of an underworld devil somewhere. She wore a matching black hennin that gave her the appearance of being the regal and unholy bride of that underworld devil (for those not up to date on the latest fashion trends of evil noblewomen, a hennin is a tall, cone-shaped headdress that is as impractical as it is vertical (and they are *very* vertical)).

It was a slow day at the shop, and Maribella and Asteria had been sitting at the rear fireplace having a rest. Maribella shot up when the new guests arrived.

Lady Malicent stood straight and silent. She had a bosom that rose and fell like a poorly-planned revolution.

"Good day, miss," said Maribella, and she fought the urge to curtsy. "How can I help you today?"

"You can't," said Lady Malicent. Her voice was as cold as the rest of her, and it carried a demanding tone. "To think I could attain any help from the likes of you implies you have some sort of worth."

"Well that's rather rude," said Maribella.

"What you *can* do is help yourself by leaving this place at once," said Malicent.

"And why would I want to go and do a thing like that?"

Asteria added in, "The foreboding books with the talking and the warnings have already been dealt with. We are in no danger. Bookshop is quite safe."

"I'm sorry," said Malicent, her eyes on Maribella, "but was an inbred ox just now trying to talk? I could have sworn I heard something that sounded just like that."

"Well my *word*," said Maribella.

"You should leave this place, little girl, because you don't own it. I do."

"I'm sorry, there must be some confusion. My name is Maribella Waters."

"I don't care what your name is."

"Well you should, because I'm the owner of this bookshop. I corresponded with Baron Blauca himself via letter. The deed was purchased, the payment sent, the keys handed over."

"Baron Blauca is a close, personal friend of mine who sometimes makes administrative mistakes. If he sold you this building, he was in error."

"We'd just have to take that up with Baron Blauca, wouldn't we?"

"There is no need. I have the true deed right here. Miles." She snapped her fingers and her muscled man stepped forward and slapped down a parchment onto the front desk where sales were made. Apparently the man's name was Miles, and Malicent wasn't just randomly proclaiming a unit of measurement.

Maribella stooped over the paper, reading it quickly, finger tracing line by line. "Hmm, well, I'm a bit confused..."

"Must you insist on wasting words on the obvious?" said Malicent.

"...because it looks here like you only own the *land* that this building is built on. This building, and a few of its neighbors."

"This is true."

"But I own the building itself."

"Land ownership supersedes any ownership of property built on it."

"I'd have to double check the laws on that point. Sounds a bit flimsy."

"The codes are quite clear. You should never have been sold the building to begin with. It was a grand mistake, but not one that concerns me. It concerns *you*."

"I would think it concerns you as well, seeing as you're here being quite rude to me and my friend."

"I'm here to educate you on reality, and to suggest to you

that you vacate these premises as soon as possible."

"Well I don't think I'll be doing that at all."

It was at this point that Miles the muscled man walked forward and cracked his knuckles and spoke up in a voice that sounded like a drunken toad. "You'd better think of doing it, missy, because things could get real ugly for you real quick if you don't."

"Is that a threat?" asked Maribella. "Or by 'get real ugly real quick', you're referring to your face? The Cozy Quill has its own guard, so I'm not impressed."

"That so?" said Miles, and he turned to Asteria where she sat. "Is that what this lady right here is supposed to be? Am I supposed to be afraid of a woman?" He strode over to the chairs, his walk as casual as his sexism.

And then Asteria stood up.

And Miles craned his head up, and up, and up.

"This is correct assumption," said Asteria. "You are supposed to be much afraid of me."

Miles cleared his throat and smoothly walked back behind his mistress, his head bobbing along the way just to let everyone know he was calm and relaxed and not at all suddenly terrified.

Lady Malicent sighed, showing the barest hint of an emotion other than cold derision. "If it's to come to that, I have an endless supply of goons under my pay."

"Goons?" whispered Miles, insult on his face.

"Your giant of a Ha-Mazan warrior is impressive, but don't think you'd ever win a contest of might with the likes of me. I run this town, you must know. The Baron is officially in charge, but I am effectively so. What I say happens. And what I say is that you will vacate this building."

"And what if we don't?" asked Maribella.

Lady Malicent placed her hands on her hips, glared down at Maribella, and breathed in deeply. Her bosom rose like corn prices during a drought.

"I am a generous woman," she said, her words slow and deliberate. "I will give you one week to make your preparations and leave this place. This is a kindness on my part. I do not have to do this. You may even take anything you like, including these wretched books. In exactly one week's time, whether you are here or not, my men will tear this building to the ground."

"Oh! Tear it to the ground! Why that's awful. Why would you want to go and do a thing like tear down a perfectly good building?"

"Because Leafhaven is a booming town. More people are moving here every day. It needs tiny, overpriced tenements, not bookshops."

"Tiny, overpriced tenements?"

"Yes. I plan on building tiny, overpriced tenements on this land, with the cheapest materials possible, as small as possible so I may fit as many people into the lot as I can, and then charge an exuberant amount of money for people to rent them. And they'll have to pay, because nobody else is building but me."

With that, Lady Malicent twirled about with a dramatic flair, the skirts of her hennin fluttering outward, and she and Miles left the bookshop.

And so now, only at the end of this dreadful conversation, do you, dear reader, fully understand the extent of Lady Malicent's villainy.

She was a landlord.

Chapter 10

Maribella and Asteria Read Some Books

Maribella tried to contact Baron Blauca for days. He owned a large manor in the rich part of town (you could tell it was the rich part of town because the decorative pumpkins were all giant). He had guards posted at the front gates and none of them would allow Maribella in no matter how she pleaded her case. She even brought along Asteria just on the chance she'd put some fear into them, but it was no use.

"Oh, not many people get to see Baron Blauca," said Captain Hargle one day at the Town Guard barracks as he flipped through a book. "At least no regular townsfolk. He meets with his kind often enough—that being other nobles, mind you—but he doesn't give audience to us normal people very often."

"Well that's absurd," said Maribella. "How is anyone supposed to get anything done with leadership like that? Is there truly nothing the Town Guard can do? Lady Malicent threatened to tear down the Cozy Quill with me and Asteria inside it."

Hargle shrugged. "There's nothing I can do. Them kinda laws are outside Hargle's comprehension. I'm more of a drunken-tavern-brawl-stopper kind of enforcement officer, not a property rights one. You'll have to get the Baron's attention to help with this."

While reading at the front desk one day, Maribella realized she had been going about it all wrong. She had corresponded with Baron Blauca via letter to buy the shop, so why not ask for his help in the very same way? She wrote a letter and sent it to his manor, explaining everything in detail. When she didn't get a response she sent another, and then another.

"It's very unlike the Baron to ignore these letters," she said to Clarence the oldest man in town inside the shop one day. "He was quick to reply when I was purchasing the bookshop."

Clarence shrugged as he drank tea and flipped some pages to a book. "You were probably dealing with a chancery, or secretary or bookkeeper of some such. They are known to make grievous mistakes, after all." (This might seem a cruel thing for a kindly old man like Clarence to say, but in actually he was correct. Bookkeepers often make horrible mistakes, and it's a wonder most of them were ever given the job to begin with.) "If the Blauca family was wanting to offload the bookshop, it's no wonder they got back to you quickly then. They wanted your money. Now that the ink has settled, I wouldn't expect much help."

"Oh bother, but what do I do?" Maribella worried at the corner of a book. "It's already been several days. The week is almost up."

Dave the doorman at the entrance to the Bloody Stump didn't have any answers either. "Don't ask me," he said helpfully.

"But is what Lady Malicent said true?" asked Maribella, wrapping her Complimentary Mysterious Cloak tighter. "You know how these underhanded things go. Does the Baron really just do whatever she asks?"

Dave leaned in closer, whispering and looking over his shoulder. "Rumor is, that's how it goes. She's got the man under her thumb, and she's the one who really owns this town."

"Oh *bother*."

Asteria had her own idea on how to handle Lady Malicent and her army of goons.

"I will now proceed to destroy them all," she said while gripping her battle axe.

"You will do *no* such thing!" said Maribella.

"Why?"

"Because violence isn't the answer."

Asteria narrowed her eyes and looked to the side, as if lost in confusion.

"Besides, there are too many of them for you," said Maribella.

"This is not true. I have ability to slaughter many men at once. I am seven-foot Ha-Mazan woman with many muscles, they are southern men."

"There are too many. Even considering how big and strong you are, they would swarm you."

"You could help me in battle. Lower numbers. Help make fight fair."

"I most certainly could not. First, I wouldn't want to, and second, I would be no help at all in a fight."

"You could be of great use. You can carry out table-for-sale trick."

"Table-for-sale trick?"

"Yes. It is classic Ha-Mazan stratagem for those not blessed with muscles to wield great and mighty weapon. You see table there?" She pointed to a small table meant for one or two people near the wall. "You grab table, approach your enemy with friendly smile on face. You say as you approach, 'hello good sir, I have fine table I wish to sell. Would you be so good as to look at it and purchase?' And then when he looks at table, you strike him in face with table. You can do this with one of Malicent's men while I handle others."

"My *goodness*."

"Table-for-sale trick never fails. You will do this thing."

"I certainly won't. But...what if they're actually interested in buying the table?"

"That is especially good fortune. You strike them with table edge right in face."

"That seems awfully cruel. What if they don't want to buy the table?"

"You strike them with table edge right in face."

"What if they know it's a trick?"

"You strike them with table edge right in face."

"It's a pretty straightforward plan, hmm?"

"This is so. No matter reaction of enemy, you strike them with table edge right in face."

"Well, there will be no table-for-sale tricks going on anywhere around this bookshop, is that understood?"

Asteria shrugged. "I will keep table close, just in case."

It grew late one day, the sun low, the sky dark, and Maribella stood next to Asteria in the empty display area at the front of the shop, looking out the windows at the street. A blustery wind blew hard and cold down the cobblestones, sending more and more colorful leaves fluttering, and nobody seemed to be out at this hour.

Maribella drank some hot tea and pulled her shawl tighter. "It's cold and windy out today," she said. "Let's stay inside and read books."

"Hmm?" said Asteria. "I do not read. This has been well established."

"I know. Come along. I'll read them to you."

Minutes later the women were situated at the fire in the back of the main floor. Maribella pulled the chairs next to each other and motioned for Asteria to sit down.

"Here's your tea and your blanket," said Maribella.

"I am not cold," said Asteria. "And I do not want tea at this moment."

"If we're going to read then you'll need these items. Here, just sit there, just like that." She placed the blanket over Asteria's lap. "And set this right here." She placed the cup of steaming tea on the little table next to the giant barbarian.

"I do not understand. Why do I need these items?"

"They're for reading."

"Is not book for reading?"

"A book is the bare minimum needed for reading. But to do it properly you need these items as well. They help enhance the activity. Now look here, I went and pulled several books that I thought you may be interested in, and some that I think you should expose yourself to for your own good."

"Hmm," hummed Asteria, distrustful.

Maribella sat and adjusted her own blanket, and leaned in close toward Asteria's chair. The fire crackled happily, the tea gave off a pleasant aroma, and the outside world with all of its troubles went away.

The first book she pulled from the pile was a massive book. When I say this book was massive, I mean it was absolutely gargantuan. It could be used as an anchor for a ship at sea. A giant ship, not a little one. It could be placed in a trebuchet and flung at an enemy castle, and the entire castle would collapse to the ground upon only one impact. This was the sort of book that would sit on a rock for years, and hundreds of hopeful young men would attempt to lift it and all fail, except for that one special young man who would become the fated elected senator of the land.

Just what sort of book was this, I hear you asking? Maribella explained:

"This genre of writing is called the *epic fantasy novel.*"

"Epic fantasy novel," intoned Asteria with a sense of awe.

"Yes. These are books that involve a lot of people who carry oversized weapons like giant swords and giant axes and they go around trying to kill each other. I figured it would be right up your alley. Now I know there's no way we could finish this entire book, but we can at least read the beginning part. You may end up liking it and want to read the rest yourself."

"This sounds like a very special kind of book."

"It is. I've never read it, but this one is by one of the more famous authors of this genre, Robert Airickson R. R. R. Branderstopper."

"What do all the R's stand for?"

"I suppose 'Really, Really, Really Long'. But never mind that. Here we go."

With the atmosphere finally perfectly set, Maribella began to read.

**The Chronicle Tomes of Archived Saga Scrolls
Book One of Twenty-Seven
A Blade of Blood and Guts**

*Forward One of Prologue One of Part One
The Year 21,492 A.D.F.E.
The Hyperion Planet Cluster
Rhy'Ghar
The Empire of Blor'Rhun
The City of Blur'Ghen
Early Morning*

And so it was in the days of King-Lord-God M'Shran'Lhan that the Crab Emperor did battle in direct contest with his Blood Orb seated firmly in the Cren'Rhan. The Fifth Epoch of the Lon'Dran Festival of the Sea was in full blarnen *when Ed'Rich the Champion of the Crab Emperor did join the Temple of Drunjen, where all the City of the Lost had gathered this fateful day. It had been thirty-seven thousand hundred years since the last Fifth Epoc of the Lon'Dran Festival of the Sea, and the peoples of Blor'Rhun were indeed fraught with upheaval on account of the raging* melarkies *in the Great Eastern Expanse of Dren'Jhun'Hhub'Eirt...*

"...erht...eeh...gree hee ah...aite?" sounded out Maribella. "Uh, let's just skip on ahead..."

And so now follows the ponderous histories and culture of the Undermud peoples and their thousand year Anguish against the Wallows of Insufferabilities, starting with the founder from the year 20,514 A.D.F.E. and ending in...

"Uh," said Maribella, and looked up at Asteria.

"I have no idea what is happening and I do not understand what any of these words mean," said Asteria. "I must be very illiterate indeed."

"Actually, don't sell yourself short. I'm just as confused as you are." She tossed the book onto the floor and three buildings down Clarence the oldest man in town thought lightning had struck his home.

"I thought it was about swinging around swords and killing people," said Asteria.

"I did too. Maybe it gets there eventually, but just needs a bit of backstory for it all to make sense. Here, I went about this all completely the wrong way. I started us off with advanced writing when we should have started simple. What we need is a good short story, and I have just the one."

She opened up a reasonably-sized book and placed it between them.

"This book is actually a collection of short stories, and it's called *The Collected Short Stories of Eustace Hemingwoh*. He was a very well-respected and famous author for excelling at the minimalism style of writing. I thought that you may appreciate minimalism, because it uses less words than other styles of writing."

"Yes, I like minimalism," said Asteria with solemn sincerity.

"Here, this is one of his most famous short stories." Maribella began to read.

Hills Like Grey Baboons

The hills surrounding Plainfield were grey and ugly. It was hot, and the building made shade. The man and the girl sat outside the building. The stagecoach would come pretty soon.

"I'm thirsty," said the girl.

"So get something to drink," said the man.

"Let's drink ale," said the girl.

"Two ales, please," said the man toward the building.

But the building didn't respond, because nobody else was there.

The girl looked off into the hills. They were grey in the sun and ugly.

"They look like grey baboons," said the girl.

"I've never seen one before," said the man.
"Neither have I," said the girl.
The girl sighed.
"I guess they don't really look like grey baboons after all."

Maribella's voice stopped and she flipped the page, but it was just a different story there. She looked all about, wondering if she missed something.

"Is that it?" asked Asteria.

"Huh," said Maribella. "It seems so. The story just ends here."

"Is a page missing?"

"No, it's all here."

"I do not understand. Hills do not look like baboons. Story makes no sense."

"You've seen baboons?"

"Grey baboons are common in Ha-Mazan Tribe lands. I have killed many. Never have I seen one who looks like hill."

"Huh. Well, I guess it's more about what it makes you *feel*."

"I feel much confusion."

"But see, it's minimalism. The whole point is there is more responsibility put on us, the readers, to try to figure it all out and make sense of what the story was about. I'm sure it's loaded with symbolism as well. What does the empty building represent? What do the hills represent?"

"Grey baboons."

"No...that..." Maribella sighed. "Okay, no minimalism, then." She looked at the pile of books she had pulled and began to feel very stupid. Her face turned red and a seed of doubt began to grown in her. "This was silly," she said. "I'm sorry. We don't have to do this. You can go back to your axe exercises."

But Asteria didn't stir. Instead, there was the wonderful sound of her sipping her hot tea. "No," she said. "I am enjoying reading books. You will read me more, please and thank you."

After being stunned for a brief bit, Maribella picked up the next book.

The two women lost track of time, and read late into the night until both were very sleepy.

Chapter 11

Maribella Thinks Logically

It was early morning, and the one week was up.

"What do we do?" asked Maribella, pacing up and down the bookshop. "I still haven't heard back from the Baron. Today's the day."

"Hmm," hummed Asteria. "I will fight hired goons to the death."

"That's very kind of you Asteria, but I'd rather you not go and die."

"I will take many of them with me."

"That's not persuading me. No, we need to *outsmart* them. We need to think sideways. We need get the best of them without them expecting it. But how?"

The two women thought deeply. Maribella paced and Asteria leaned against the front desk, fingers to chin.

"Attack home of Lady Malicent," said Asteria. "She will be much caught off guard in this case, and she will break easily. I have foreseen this."

"No, no, no. I said no violence. That can't be the answer to everything."

"Hmm."

"We have to think it through logically. There's a solution to this, I know there is. We just need to lay the problem out in a clear manner and find the answer. Lady Malicent is going to have her goons tear this building down, with us in it or not. That's her primary goal. Our primary goal is to keep the building standing, and with us in it. We can't physically stop them. But can we stop them in another manner? Or rather..."

She narrowed her eyes and stood still.

"We could *protect* the building somehow. Make it impossible for the building itself to be demolished."

"Magic?"

"I don't know any magic. Do you?"

"I do not."

"Then we can't use magic. Let's see...protect the building...make it impossible for it to be torn down..."

And then that wonderful moment of realization hit Maribella. Her eyes grew wide, her heart jumped in her chest, and she twirled toward Asteria, grabbed her by the front of the tunic and began to shake her.

"The goblins!" she cried. "The goblins, Asteria!"

"What about them?"

"They're an endangered species! If we invite them back into the bookshop, then it would be clearly illegal for Malicent to tear down the building. The entire town would be against them. Everyone here loves goblins apparently." (Reference Chapter Two: Maribella Hires a Murder-Hobo.) "We get the goblins back, spread the word around town so everyone knows they're living here, then it'll be impossible for Malicent to make a move on the bookshop."

"Hmm," said Asteria, and she lifted her chiseled chin and rubbed at it. "This plan is good plan. Maribella is wise woman."

"I know! So the only issue is we have to find them. Where did they go?"

Asteria shrugged. "I do not know. The goblins I chased out spread like disease during courting season. I tossed leader goblin very far."

"Well then come on, we've got to search the town."

And search the town they did. They searched high and low, down every alleyway, in every nook and cranny. They interviewed everyone they knew, and with each interview they were led down a hopeful path.

"Goblins like water," said Captain Hargle. "Go down to the river and see if they're about there. Maybe my brother has seen them."

They checked the docks, but there were no goblins to be found. They did find Captain Bargle, though. We haven't met Bargle yet, but just imagine the spitting image of Hargle, except far fishier in both smell and character.

"I ain't seen no goblins here," he said, scratching his beard. "They like dark places. Check the south side alleyways and the dank taverns there."

They checked the southern alleyways and the dank taverns, but found no goblins. They did find Dave the doorman, though.

"No goblins have been in here," he said, and then leaned forward to whisper a secret. "Rumor is, all the goblins left town. Right about when you arrived, in fact. Went yelling up the road, never to be seen again."

The search had taken all day. What was once elation was now deflation. Maribella walked back to the Cozy Quill with her shoulders slumped.

I expect Malicent's goons will already be working on the bookshop when we get back, she thought, kicking a rock. *Today was the day, after all.*

"This plan was foolish," she said as they approached the turn that led to the shop. "We wasted the whole day on a goose chase while we could have been gathering our things and getting as many books out as we could. Now look at us."

"It will be okay, Bell," said Asteria.

Maribella looked up at her. "What did you call me?"

"There you are, Maribella!" cried Clarence the oldest man in town. He had been waiting on the Cozy Quill's porch, leaning on both canes. "Where have you been? I wanted to do so some browsing today, and the shop is closed."

"I'm afraid it won't be open for long," said Maribella.

"Oh? Why's that?"

"Lady Malicent owns the land it's built on, apparently, and she's going to tear it down today."

Clarence the oldest man in town sagely nodded his head. "Ah, the little Lady Malicent, eh?"

"I didn't find very much about her that was little, her ego most of all."

"Oh, but I remember her as being very little, once upon a time. A lonely girl with no friends who liked to stay inside. Her parents were never kind to her, or so I heard."

"Well that's a very tragic backstory and as you can see I'm just all glowing with empathy for her, but that doesn't stop the fact that she's a witch of a grown woman now and she's going to tear down my bookshop."

"That's quite the predicament to be in." Clarence shook his head, clicking his tongue. "If only there was something I could do for you."

"I did have a plan," said Maribella, sitting down on a barrel on the porch.

"Oh?"

"Yes. I was going to find those goblins I ran out before and move them back in. This building would be a protected landmark in that case. The King's law would make it so. But the goblins all left town."

"They did, they did..."

"So the plan is a bust."

"...all except for the laziest one."

Maribella blinked. She looked up at Clarence. "What was that?"

"I said you're right, they all left town to go live in the forest. All of them except for the laziest one. The goblin girl."

Maribella hopped off the barrel. "The goblin girl? Gidget? She's still in town?"

"Close enough, sure. Just on the outskirts, by the apple orchard. There's a hill just outside of town near the road, and up on that hill stands a single giant apple tree. Travelers have been telling stories of a lone goblin girl sleeping underneath that tree all day and all night. She's right there, Maribella. All you have to do is go and get her."

Maribella lit up in a smile. She would have shaken the old man in her excitement, but she didn't want to murder him, so instead she shook Asteria again.

"The goblin girl!" said Maribella. "Gidget the Goblin Girl is still in town!"

Chapter 12

Gidget Becomes a Deity

"**D**o you see it, Asteria?" asked Maribella, tugging Asteria along. "Is it not the most beautiful apple tree you've ever seen?"

It quite was. A giant, as far as apple trees go, and situated at the very top of a perfectly green hill. Behind this hill was an endless sky the color of gold. The setting sun shone against elaborate clouds built on top of one another, and it seemed as if a celestial city hung in the atmosphere above the hill and the apple tree.

And there, a teeny, tiny dark speck reclined motionless beneath the tree.

"Come along," said Maribella, and together she and Asteria climbed the hill.

The air was cold as usual, but it grew calm up on the hill. The world became silent. The hustle and bustle of Leafhaven was far away. No voices clucking, no hoofs clopping, no hammers clacking. Even the sound of bristling leaves went away. Maribella stopped and looked back at one point, and she could see the entire town sprawl beneath her, along with the flowing river and the nearby forest and green fields and the farms and the pumpkin patches and the mountains in the far distance. All of these sensations combined together to create something surreal, as if she had stepped into a dream, and a rather pleasant one at that.

"There," whispered an awe-struck Asteria. "Just ahead. The goblin girl."

Maribella walked the last several feet and stood beneath the apple tree. Gidget the Goblin Girl lay on her back in the grass, fast asleep, snoring peacefully with an open mouth. Dozens of little sharp teeth were on display, and she twitched every once in a while. She looked so relaxed that Maribella envied her. It was the kind of sleep that each and every one of us would be thankful to have.

Maribella looked up. She just now noticed that the apple tree had no apples left. It had already been harvested, of course.

All except for a single last apple, hanging precariously above Gidget.

Maribella cleared her throat and took a step forward. "Hello there. Miss goblin? Miss Gidget? Are you awake?"

Gidget continued to peacefully snore.

"Do you want me to nudge her?" asked Asteria.

"No," said Maribella. "She snapped last time I tried that. And I don't want to frighten her either."

"I do not think this one has ever been frightened."

Maribella cleared her throat even louder. "Gidget, I'm sorry to wake you, but—"

The goblin stirred, smacking her lips, but her eyes didn't open. Her head slightly swiveled, and a little voice came out her big mouth. "A lozenge will help that throat."

And then she went right back to snoring.

"Wha..." Maribella looked to Asteria, who shrugged.

I didn't come all this way to leave empty-handed, thought Maribella. She braced herself and stood right next to the goblin.

"Gidget," she said. "Would you like to come back to the bookshop and live with us?"

A short, high-pitched sound came from Gidget's mouth, and her shoulders gave the barest hint of a shrug.

"I'm not sure you heard me clearly," said Maribella. "I asked if you would like to come back to the Cozy Quill and live with us. You can stay there for as long as you like."

"Eh," came the sound again, evolving from its original indistinguishable form. The second shrug that came was a little higher quality too.

"We would of course feed you—"

"Okay," said Gidget, eyes still closed, still sprawled with her limbs out, breath still coming in the slow and gentle repetitions of sleep.

Maribella was a bit confused. "You'll...come back to town and live with us?"

"Sure."

"Just like that, without even asking about why we want you back or anything?"

"Meh."

Maribella looked to Asteria. "She wants to come back. I guess this is going to work out after all."

And then came the command.

It came in the form of a gentle whisper.

"Carry me."

The women looked back to the goblin, still sleeping. "Did...did she tell us to carry her back?" asked Maribella.

"This is true," said Asteria.

"All right, then. That's simple enough. Asteria? Could you carry her?"

Asteria strode forward, but then Gidget lifted a single clawed finger. "Wait one moment."

The two women stood motionless, their eyes shifting. Maribella began to think the goblin had fallen back into a deep sleep. "Gidget—"

"*Shhh*," whispered Gidget, and then a long, drawn out whisper: "*Waaaiiiit for iiiiit.*"

They all waited in total silence and tranquility.

The gentlest wind to have ever blown blew.

It was enough to cause the last apple of the season to fall from the tree.

The apple fell directly down toward Gidget.

Gidget allowed her jaw to relax.

The apple landed in her mouth.

She began to chew and swallow.

It was all done without any superfluous movement by the goblin.

Maribella slapped the top of her head. "That was *extraordinary!* You deliberately chose this spot. You...you waited all this time. You...well you knew that the wind would blow. That was the most magnificent, amazing display of laziness I've ever seen!"

"I am most impressed," said Asteria in awe.

"It's as if you've turned laziness into an art," said Maribella. "You've maximized the efficiency of doing nothing yet still gaining benefit. I...I'm simply blown away."

Gidget swallowed the last bit of apple, then simply lifted her arms. "Learn from me."

"Right away," said Maribella. "Asteria, lift her up. Let's get back to Leafhaven as quick as we can."

Asteria transported the goblin as if she were an infant, and Gidget slept on the way back to the bookshop. Once there, Maribella was happy to find the building still unaccosted.

"Where shall we place her?" asked Asteria as they closed the door behind them. "How will we get word out that we have little sleepy goblin here?"

"We put her in the display window," said Maribella, madly grabbing a table and tossing books off it. She dragged it to the empty display area in the front window. This space pressed outward toward the street a few feet, so that things of interest could be set there and passersby could look in at them.

Gidget was going to be a permanent thing of interest.

"Here we are," said Maribella, propping up the table with books under two legs so that it faced the windows. They pushed it right up against the window, and Asteria placed the sleeping goblin onto it.

"It's perfect," said Maribella, admiring their work. Gidget slept peacefully on the table, exposed to the entire world passing by outside. "Would you like a pillow or blanket?" asked

Maribella.

"No, no," whispered Gidget. "Goblins run hot." She smacked her lips a few times and began to snore, her head tilted back, her arms splayed out wantonly.

Maribella grabbed a bell and dashed outside. She would waste no time. The bell caught people's attention, and her voice cried out loud and clear. "Come and see the goblin of the Cozy Quill Bookshop! Gather 'round for free and admire a rare and endangered creature in the flesh! Gidget the Goblin Girl is here for your viewing pleasure! Witness her majesty in all its goblin glory! Come one and come all!"

It worked. Townspeople of all walks of life gathered around, craning their heads to see the sleeping goblin through the window.

"Well would you look at that," said one.

"A real life goblin, in the flesh," said another.

"They're good luck, they are."

"Once they find a spot they like, they don't like to move."

"The Cozy Quill is a lucky spot from here on out, then!"

"It's a landmark now, you can be sure of that."

"Go and get the kids, they'll want to see."

Gidget slightly stirred in her display, as if just now becoming aware of what was happening. Maribella froze, unable to breathe as she watched the goblin.

What if she despises everything about this situation? thought Maribella. *What if she resents being a prop and gets angry and runs off?*

With heavy lids and lethargic body, Gidget uttered a single phrase:

"I am your deity."

Maribella smiled and clapped her hands together. She clung to Asteria's side, who was smiling herself. "It's working, Asteria."

"Hah," said Asteria. "Who would have thunk one little goblin would lead to all this?"

"Oh, but we'll need to make a sign or something. Some

kind of advertisement with her name above it. 'Gidget the Goblin Wonder'. Something like that. But oh! There are some grapes in the pantry, weren't there? You should feed Gidget, Asteria. The people will like that. One grape at a time, so that her big mouth snaps like it does. Just watch your fingers."

And so on it went. The crowd grew bigger and bigger, and of course people wanted to come inside the shop to see as well.

"Only admire the goblin via the window viewing area, please!" called Maribella. "But by all means, do some shopping while you're here if you'd like."

After several minutes of pure joy, the crowd began to quiet, and from the very back it parted slowly. Eventually, the woman who was the very opposite of pure joy appeared in all her icy darkness.

She had more than one goon with her this time. Lots more, in fact.

She stood in front of the window, arms at her sides, shoulders back and posture pristine and perfect, her hennin high and mighty. Her eyes glared into the window at the sleeping goblin.

Lady Malicent took a deep breath, and her bosom inflated like the housing prices she so wished to impose on Leafhaven.

We have officially reached the point in the story where there will be no more bosom metaphors. Three maximum are all that's allowed. Many of you will be thankful and let out sighs of relief. Some of you may be saddened. Such is life.

"What," said Lady Malicent. "Is. This. Wretched. Thing."

"It's a goblin girl," said Maribella.

"I can see that."

"Oh, then why ask—"

"What is it doing on my property?"

"The building is my property actually—"

"What is it doing inside the building?"

Maribella looked to the window and peered inside. Then looked back up to Lady Malicent, crossed her arms and nodded. "Napping."

Lady Malicent simmered. That is, she was a few degrees away from boiling. She lifted a hand and snapped her fingers. "Remove the goblin from the premises."

Led by Miles the lead goon, her group of ruffians marched forward with clubs in hands. The crowd surged against them.

"*Hey!*" cried an exceptionally impassioned man. "You can't go moving a goblin from where it's sleeping. That's against the law."

"Yeah," shouted his friend. "That little goblin in there didn't do nothin' to the likes of you. All she wants to do is sleep and be comfortable, and then some rich noble like yourself wants to come and move everything around. Well not today!"

"Yeah!" shouted a woman. "The King's decree is very clear on the matter. You're not to disturb or move a goblin wherever it may be."

Malicent's simmering grew to a steady boil. "I am preparing this building for destruction first thing tomorrow morning. I must remove the goblin if the building is to be destroyed."

"You're doing no such thing," said another townsperson. This man had a tear in his eye as if he had known Gidget his whole life. "I love that little goblin, god help me, and she didn't do nothin' to nobody."

"That building is a protected landmark!" cried yet another man, angrily pointing his finger at the Cozy Quill. Spittle flew from his mouth as he shouted, such was his passion, and his face went bright red. "You're not to lay a finger on it, or god help you. If one plank or board is torn from its side, we'll know it was you, Lady Malicent!"

"Yeah, Lady Malicent!"

"I love that little goblin!"

"That little goblin is my hero!"

"Go on and get going, Lady Malicent!"

"Yeah, get going! Nobody wants you here!"

And then came the pumpkins. Dozens upon dozens of pumpkins in all shapes and sizes were flung at the group of goons, cracking open over their backs. The seeds and insides were thrown as well, and one big handful splattered directly onto Lady Malicent's dress. Maribella looked on in stunned awe.

Well I don't approve of the pumpkin-throwing, she thought. *But besides that, this went better than I ever could have imagined.*

And then, snapping her out of her reverie, Lady Malicent *spun* on Maribella in a violent twirl and clenched her trembling fist in a ball so tight it might have burst. The noblewoman's face was a twisted painting of anger and hatred, and she snarled as she spoke. The sudden display of fierce emotion coming from such a normally calm and cool woman was outright terrifying.

"This won't be the end of it, little girl. I'll tell the Baron about this at once, and *then you'll see.*"

Maribella waved goodbye as Malicent stumbled down the street, slipping on pumpkin skins. "Always a pleasure!"

Chapter 13

Leafhaven Celebrates Duckover

It was time for a celebration. A festival celebration, in fact. One of the most marvelous celebrations of the year. That's right. You know the one. It's everyone's favorite.

Duckover.

"Duckover?" asked Asteria, scrunching up her brows.

"Yes, Duckover," said Maribella, preparing her lantern on the front desk of the shop. "You don't celebrate Duckover in the Ha-Mazan Tribes?"

"We do no such thing. We eat ducks. We do not celebrate them."

"Well I'm sure some people here eat ducks as well, but that's not what Duckover is about. It's that magical time of the year when ducks fill the sky, traveling over the region as they migrate south. Ducks are considered very good luck, you know. You should never feed a duck bread, by the way, and in fact you shouldn't feed them much at all, because if you do then they might be late in their migrations and that's just not good for anybody."

Maribella was quite correct in her warning, and so you, dear reader, should take heed. Don't feed the ducks.

(But if you must, go with cracked corn, birdseed, or oats.)

Asteria struggled with her own lantern. She couldn't seem to put it together correctly. "I do not understand. Waterfowl are angry and vicious, and they will do battle like Ha-Mazan warriors. Why venerate them?"

"Well perhaps the ducks up where you live are a bit stressed out so they're angry, but down here ducks bring good fortune. They also carry wishes of good fortune abroad, which is how Duckover came to be. That's what these lanterns are for, you see."

"To symbolize our wishes and good fortune?"

"That's quite right. The ducks will take our tidings and bring them south."

"And how does this benefit us?"

"Well..." Maribella was just a bit caught off guard. Nobody had ever asked that before. "It doesn't, I suppose. The wishes and good fortunes travel to the south. To the people there."

"Hmm," pondered Asteria.

"And then later in the spring, the people in the south also celebrate Duckover, and their wishes and good fortune travel up to us. The whole idea is to help each other instead of ourselves."

"And what if flying duck runs into floating lantern and crashes and is set aflame?"

"Oh, that's considered especially lucky then. The lantern owner eats roast duck for dinner."

And then came the mighty sigh from Dave the forlorn doorman, who had been sitting right there with the two women constructing his own lantern.

"What's wrong, Dave?" asked Maribella. "You sound more forlorn than usual."

"Oh, nothing really," he said.

"It is the confusing lantern construction, yes?" said Asteria.

"No, that's not it. I finished that a long time ago." He held up his perfect lantern. "It's just, I've been so lonely lately."

"Lonely?" said Maribella. "But you meet all kinds of people at the Bloody Stump. You're surrounded by them, in fact."

Dave sighed heavily and rested his chin in his hand. "You've never been alone in a crowd? That's my life. Doorman Dave. Everyone knows me, but nobody really does. They pass by and nod their head, but none of them stop to talk. I'm just there to hand out cloaks and wallop somebody when they get too rowdy. And worst of all, there's not a hint of a lady in my life. That's right. It's that bad. I'm maidenless."

"Oh, dear," said Maribella. "Well, I don't think we could help you with that. But...perhaps Duckover will bring good luck?"

"The luck comes on the way back up from the south. The Ha-Mazan Tribes don't celebrate Duckover, like Asteria here said. There'll be no good wishes for me on their wings until spring."

"Well perhaps it'll happen anyway. But come along, Dave. You can go to the festival with us this year."

Maribella helped Asteria finish her lantern, and together the trio went out into town. "Are you sure you'll be fine here alone?" asked Maribella to Gidget, who was currently sleeping on her display table. She simply snored in response, and so Maribella took that as a yes.

The streets were lively with celebration. Bands played flutes and lutes and banged on drums while people danced. Food vendors sprang up everywhere, and Maribella had to stop as Asteria got a little bit from each one. After all, a woman her size could eat a lot.

"Never have I tasted such abundant food," she said, savoring some marinated chicken on a stick. "Duckover is my favorite celebration."

Maribella led them to Peabush Square, the center of Leafhaven, to find the space filled with most of the town. Children ran and played, passionate minstrels sang to enraptured crowds, acrobats sprang into the air and tumbled. Most everyone held lanterns in anticipation.

Usually, the lord of a town was the one to say some words and officially call for the release of the lanterns, and Maribella had been eager to see if she could catch Baron Blauca in the event. But she soon learned that he never attended these things, and so as the sun sank below the horizon and twilight covered the world in its magical and melancholy air, it was Captain

Hargle who clambered up to the raised wooden platform.

"Another year behind us," he called to the crowd, "and another Duckover upon us. The seasons change from warm to cold to warm, and the ducks do so ever fly to where it is good and comfortable, as is the way of the world. And so with them we send our wishes, our good fortunes, our dreams and our love. We light these lanterns and imbue them with these tidings, and send them south with those brave ducks, ever flying, ever moving, ever hopeful."

Silence swept over the crowd, and a large mass of ducks just then flew overhead in a great V-pattern. Captain Hargle let go of his lantern, and the rest of the town followed. It was a wondrous sight watching that great mass of lights filling the sky in calm silence.

Maribella, Asteria and Dave watched as their trio of little lamps reached higher and joined the others. The ducks passed overhead. For several minutes, nobody said a word.

Asteria was the first to bring her gaze from the sky. She looked around and checked over her shoulder and scanned the horizon and looked Dave up and down. "Has it worked?" she asked him. "Do you now have girlfriend?"

Dave looked around as well. "I don't think so."

Maribella couldn't help but wince. "I'm...not sure it works quite like that. The ducks aren't magic."

"Oh," said Asteria, looking back up.

"But they're a symbol of hope. And that's the important thing to get out of this."

And just like the, a conch shell horn sounded loud and clear from outside town.

Asteria's brows rose high in alarm. "This sounds like army call. Is town under attack?"

Maribella smiled. "Not in the least. It's much better than that. He's finally here, and perfect timing too. On Duckover of all days!"

"Who is here?"

"The Llama Merchant." She nodded. "And my first order of

new book stock."

Chapter 14

The Llama Merchant Comes to Leafhaven

"**A**h, here we are," said Maribella, standing on the front porch of the Cozy Quill. She and Asteria looked down the street as the first of the llamas appeared around the corner. A small figure sat on top of this llama, and behind the pair walked another llama, and behind that llama was another llama, and so on and so forth, and it seemed as if reality now consisted of an infinite supply of llamas walking in a line forever until they finally stopped appearing and a total of ten llamas slowly walked down Main Street.

Do you know much about llamas? They're marvelous creatures. Did you know they can carry about thirty percent of their body weight? That's nearly one third! It's no wonder they make desirable pack animals. Not to mention llamas are majestic creatures with pleasant, happy faces and wonderful haircuts. The next time you come across a llama, tell it "good day" and watch as it beams at you with approval.

There exists a myth that involves a Heavenly Llama who is said to drink water from the ocean and urinate rain. Thankfully this myth is completely untrue.

Oh, llamas! They're lovely. In fact, the llama may very well just be the greatest animal in the world. They can do everything. They make wonderful pets due to their friendly disposition. There are even guard llamas who stand guard over flocks of their smaller friends such as sheep and the inferior alpaca (vastly overrated imitations of llamas). Many a dog has been reduced to depression after learning a guard llama has taken its job.

But that's enough about llamas in general. Let's get specific. The Llama Merchant's llamas were very large, and so their packs were very great. Goods were piled up high, secured by ropes, and llamas in the line followed the lead llama without the need for a tether to keep them all together. Although they had traveled many miles, they didn't appear tired or haggard or dying at all. They walked with the calm confidence of an animal that knows its worth.

They were sport llamas, you see. Bred for performance.

"A nomadic merchant," said Asteria. "We have them in the north, but never have I seen one with llama before."

"Oh yes, the Llama Merchant is famous around these parts. He travels all over the place, making trades and delivering goods. I used to buy things from him before I moved. I sent an order by mail a while ago to a stop on his route, so he should have some books for me."

"I see. So this is how it happens."

Maribella looked up at Asteria. "Come again?"

"The resupply of books. A wondrous thing, and it is done via llama."

"Well, sometimes it's done via llama."

The Llama Merchant slowly drew closer, and Maribella was quite surprised to see a small young woman, possibly no more than a teenager, sitting atop the lead llama. She wore a coat of llama fur with a big hood on top, and at her shoulder clung a strange little furry creature the likes Maribella had never seen before.

"Huh," said Maribella. "Is...is that the Llama Merchant?"

"Did you not say you buy from him—er, her, before?"

"Well, yes, I have purchased some things from the Llama Merchant before, but I've never actually met her."

Asteria blinked a few times, thinking. "How is this thing possible? Buy without ever meeting?"

Maribella fidgeted. "Well, never mind all that. Here she is."

She stepped forward and waved and gave a friendly smile. "Hello there! Are you the Llama Merchant?"

The young woman was indeed possibly just a teenager and a diminutive one at that, and it was surprising to see someone so young in charge of such a great burden. The animal clinging to her looked like some sort of deformed monkey. It had grey hair with long arms, and black fur over its eyes, and it seemed to be perpetually smiling. It moved extremely slow. In fact, it exuded a calmness that permeated the entire caravan. The creature was calm, the llamas were calm, and the girl was calm.

She slowly turned around in her saddle (the strange creature followed her every movement), looked at the line of nine llamas standing patiently, and then slowly turned back to Maribella. "That would be me."

"Oh, well it's a pleasure to meet you. I'm Maribella Waters, and this is my bookshop the Cozy Quill. I believe you have some books for me?"

"That I do." She dismounted, her movements smooth and deliberate.

Asteria stepped forward. "I am Asteria Helsdottir. Ha-Mazan warrior. It is great honor to meet you and your animals."

The Llama Merchant looked outright tiny standing under Asteria. She looked up, and her strange creature did as well, a placid smile on its face. "I'm Catalina, and this is Esteban the sloth."

"Hello Catalina," said Asteria with a little bow. "Hello Esteban the sloth."

The sloth looked as if he approved.

"I've got your books right back here. Llama number three. Alejandro. Come along."

A few minutes later the women were inside the Cozy Quill with a stack of new books on the table. Catalina counted out coins and put them in her purse. She had handed Esteban off to Asteria, and the two of them stared into each others eyes silently.

"This is all wonderful, thank you," said Maribella, flipping through a new book.

"No problem," said Catalina. "It's what I do."

"And oh! Here it is! The entire, complete *Lady Jeanie Mysteries* collection. They're in wonderful condition." She ran her hand along a stack of similar looking books. There were a great many of them, perhaps twenty or so.

"*Lady Jeanie Mysteries*?" repeated Asteria.

"Yes. They're actually pretty old books. The author wrote most of them about twenty years ago now. They're aimed at a younger audience, and were wildly successful back then. They're a series of books that follow the same character, Lady Jeanie. She's a twelve year old noblewoman who first has an overbearing family and the town doesn't like her either, but then she solves mystery after mystery and she becomes greatly respected and loved. Each book is a different mystery. They're for kids, yes, or at least teenagers, but they're very entertaining and fun books. I read a few of them myself when I was young. I'm sure someone here will love them."

Asteria shook her head in wonder, whispering softly. "Books entirely made for children, falling stars..."

"So will you be in town long?" Maribella asked Catalina.

"A few days, at the least," said Catalina. "Might be a good place to settle down for the winter, I don't know."

"That would be a lovely thing to do, I think. Leafhaven is quite a nice town, after all."

"Always has been."

"I must say, how long have you been working as the Llama Merchant?"

"Oh, almost going on two decades now."

Maribella's eyebrows suddenly evolved a mind of their own and tried to jump off her forehead to explore what the world had to offer. "That...is very surprising. And impressive. And it's just you?"

"Just me and Esteban and the llamas."

"Was it originally a family business?"

"It was. First both my parents. Then my pa. Then just me."

"Oh. I see. Well, I do hope you'll stay in town a bit. Asteria seems to have taken to Esteban."

They looked over to see Asteria holding Esteban right up in front of her face, staring the sloth in the eyes.

"Yes, he has that sort of effect on people," said Catalina, packing away her things. "And like I said, maybe I'll stay. See what's new in town. Like that setup right over there."

She pointed and walked to the display window area where Gidget slept. "Yes, that's our goblin," explained Maribella. "Her name is Gidget. She stops the local noblewoman from tearing this establishment down."

"Well that's mighty kind of her."

"She also doubles as a wonderful attraction to pull in new customers. The townspeople like to come by and look at her for a bit, then they come in and buy a book. Here we go, she needs a feeding."

Maribella went back to grab a roast chicken drumstick and dangled it over Gidget's mouth. The great maw snapped opened and closed and the drumstick was gone, bone and all.

"She's easy enough to take care of," said Maribella. "You just dangle food over her every once in a while. She's yet to ever wake up and walk about, from what I've seen."

Catalina tapped her chin. "Hmm. I've got an idea that may get you a few extra coins a day, if you like."

"Oh? What'd you have in mind?"

"I could build an add-on to your display here."

"An add-on? You could build it?"

"That's right. See, I'm like my llamas—I can do a bit of everything. I've dabbled in carpentry and engineering, and I could build a machine here at the window that could add some income in your pocket."

"Well that would be lovely."

"I'd just require a small fee of course. It would take about a day to build. How about it, should I come by tomorrow morning?"

"Please do."

Asteria reluctantly gave Esteban back, and the Llama Merchant left for the night. The next morning she arrived as she said she would, only this time she had a few llamas only and they carried carpentry materials.

Maribella walked outside to find Asteria standing in the street watching Catalina work. "Morning, Asteria."

Asteria turned to her, and Maribella flinched to see Esteban hanging onto her. She was petting him, and his arms wrapped around her neck, his smug face smiling down at Maribella as if to say, "Jealous?"

"Good morning," said Asteria. "Llama girl has been working hard all morning."

"Indeed she has." It was only a bit worrying to see parts of her beloved building torn or cut, a window removed and replaced with a length of wood, and a bizarre wooden contraption slowly taking shape. Soon a great lever came out of the wall outside the building, and there was a little slot by the lever. Catalina then went inside the building and worked around and above Gidget. "What in the world is she doing?"

"Firing an arrow directly into my heart, that's what," said Dave from behind. Maribella flinched again. That morning was a morning of suddenly seeing characters she hadn't expected to see, apparently.

"Well hello Dave," she said. "What are you doing here?"

"I came by to watch. Rumor was, this here Llama Merchant was working on a project for one Cozy Quill Bookshop. Oh, but look at her! I saw her last night when she arrived, but she's even more dazzling in the sunlight."

Maribella looked between Dave and Catalina a few times, then once again her eyebrows grew minds of their own. "Oh *my*. So you fancy the *Llama Merchant?*"

"Fancy? Fancy doesn't cover it. I'm in love. It was like we were fated to meet."

Asteria perked up at the mention of fate, stopping her Esteban-strokes (Esteban then slowly turned his head to glare at her). "Fate?" she repeated.

"Yes, fate. I've never seen such a beautiful, capable woman before. She's perfect."

Asteria seemed overly serious. "Fate is a powerful thing. Do not play with it, or you will not reach the stars."

Nobody seemed to pay the barbarian's strange remark much attention. Maribella gave Dave a reassuring smile. "Well then you'll just have to go and talk to her."

"Oh, no, that's completely out of the question," said Dave.

"Why do you say that?"

"Why? I'm much too afraid she'll reject me. After all, I'm just a forlorn doorman who hands out cloaks. She's...well, she's the Llama Merchant. A living legend. She would never go for someone like me."

"But you never know if you don't try."

"Oh, I do know, actually."

"That's thinking negatively. She'll be in town for at least a few days, she told me. Work up your courage and think of something to say to her. Maybe bring her some flowers? I know a good flower shop just down the street."

"Oh, well, maybe..."

He scurried to safety later as Catalina approached, dusting off her trousers. "All finished."

Thankfully the contraption she had built looked far more natural and part of the building now. It was barely noticeable if you weren't looking. Maribella went to stand outside the display window. Beside the window was the lever and a slot. Inside, above Gidget and out of sight from street view, was a large, wooden container that narrowed to a small opening.

"How do you like it?" asked Catalina.

"I'm quite sure I have no idea what it is," said Maribella.

"Have a copper bit?"

Maribella fished around in a pocket for a coin.

"Go ahead," said Catalina.

"And do what?" asked Maribella, holding the coin up.

"Put the coin in the slot."

Maribella did just so. It fit perfectly and she heard it rattle to a stop. "Now what?"

"Pull the lever."

Maribella pulled it, and there was a great mechanical clanking. The hole in the wooden container above Gidget opened up, and several grapes fell right out. The opening closed back up, but the grapes fell toward Gidget.

The goblin had been sleeping peacefully, and she still slept as her mouth snapped open and caught the grapes. She quickly chewed and swallowed, then went back to snoring.

Maribella's eyes turned into saucers. "We're going to make a fortune."

In the several days after the construction of the Lever-Activated Goblin-Feeding Apparatus (L.A.G.F.A.), Maribella's prediction proved marginally true. She collected a great many copper bits as a great many people lined up to feed the goblin. Gidget, for her part, seemed to be completely on board with it, seeing as she never once got up from her display table or even woke up at all, really.

Several days went by, and business was good. Customers were happy to look through the new stock of books, and Maribella had also grown proficient at making a good pot of tea. She was able to make a bit more money by selling this tea, which customers gladly bought and sipped while reading (this was a good way to get money from those delightful breed of customers who enjoyed reading entire books while in the shop and then putting them back on the shelf).

"This tea is quite good," said Catalina one day. She leaned against a wall while Maribella did some upkeep on the L.A.G.F.A. "Smart of you to start selling it."

"Thank you," said Maribella, making the finishing touches on Gidget's sandwich. While the goblin girl indeed received much food through the day, it was mostly mere snacks compared to what her diet demanded, so it was still necessary to feed her whole meals regularly. This sandwich was on a long hoagie bread and filled with turkey and mustard. "This is a respectable business, after all."

"Sure. You know, you could always branch out a bit."

"Oh? How so?"

"Well I get around a lot, see. There's this town several towns over, where these two women recently started up a business selling coffee. It's apparently a huge success, and everyone is raving about it. I forget the name of it. Myths and Mugs? Champions and Cappuccinos?"

"*Coffee?*" said Maribella, scrunching up her face. "What a ridiculous idea! That would *never* work. Nobody likes coffee. Who ever thought of a mad, outlandish, nonsensical idea like selling coffee? Here you go, Gidget, open up now." She slowly fed the goblin the sandwich, starting with one end and easing the entire length in as Gidget chomped one big bite after another. "I mean really, I'll stick to my perfectly reasonable tea, thank you very much. Lagfa pull! Everyone watch your fingers!" She paused in her sandwich-feeding when a passerby inserted a coin and pulled the lever, engaging the Lever-Activated Goblin-Feeding Apparatus. Gidget caught a handful of corn kernels, many of them tumbling out the edges of her mouth. "No thank you, no selling coffee for me. Those two women, whoever they are, are headed straight for failure. It's only tried and true business practices for this entrepreneur, thank you very much." She went back to pushing the mustard and turkey sandwich down the goblin's gullet until it was completely gone and then went to go clean herself after the whole ordeal was over.

The days went by, and soon it had been a whole week since Catalina the Llama Merchant had arrived. And after this period of time she began to pack up and begin the next leg of her journey. She had unloaded her goods and she had bought up what Leafhaven had to offer (a large quantity of pumpkins, although she would have to move these fast, as pumpkin season was almost over).

Maribella and Asteria had gone out to wave Catalina off, and as the merchant girl was checking the last of her llamas, none other than Dave the doorman appeared with a bouquet of flowers in his hands.

Maribella nudged Asteria in the side. "Look at that," she whispered.

"Eh?" said Asteria.

"Dave is making his move, see?"

They were too far away to hear, but they could see Catalina's face as Dave rolled his dice. She smiled at the flowers and nodded her head some, and then she said some words to Dave, and then Dave nodded his head, and after a few more scant seconds of going back and forth Dave walked away from Catalina and Catalina pulled herself up on the lead llama with Esteban on her shoulder.

Dave walked to Maribella. "Well?" she asked. "How did it go? She took the flowers, I see."

"Yeah, she did."

He looked forlorn.

"But that was it?" asked Maribella.

"That was it. She's on her way now. On to her next travels."

The trio watched as the procession of llamas slowly began their long journey.

"This is no surprise," said Asteria. "Llama girl is going from one place to another. Llama girl has no time for making of the relationships."

They watched in silence, until Dave's small voice found its way out of him. "I waited too long. I waited too long, and now I'll live with regret."

Maribella looked up at him. His face was lacking any emotion as his eyes fixed on the llamas in the distance. "It's okay, Dave," she said. "She'll come back, after all. You can see her then."

"Oh, I may see her, sure," said Dave. "But I think that's all it'll be. She travels the world. I guard a door. That's the end of it."

Asteria crossed her arms. "Do not be sad," she said, her voice low and steady. "This is way of life. This is story of life. People come. People go. Always new faces entering your story. New faces become old faces, old faces leave. Sometimes you see again, sometimes you don't." As Maribella watched the barbarian speak, those blue eyes of hers darted down at Maribella, and then back to the horizon. "So do not be sad this face leaves, be thankful you were here to see it."

Despite her words, Maribella thought she heard sadness in Asteria's voice.

Chapter 15

Maribella and Asteria Listen to Rain

A few weeks later Maribella and Asteria decided to finish their exploration of the Cozy Quill Bookshop.

I know what you're thinking. Just how long has it been since Maribella bought the place? Shouldn't she have seen every nook and cranny so far? If you think that, you're underestimating just how large and complex of a layout the bookshop was. So many locked doors and boarded up passageways, and only so many hours in the day.

"Here we are," said Maribella, directing Asteria to smash down some boards. They stood in a second story room with a little collection books and two boarded up doorways, and Asteria began to rip apart the boards to the door on the left. Not the door on the right, that was the one that led to the room with the sentient talking worm.

After a few minutes of watching a seven-foot tall barbarian do the thing she's best at, Maribella opened the door to find not another room, but a wooden ladder placed—

What? Come again? What was that? What do you mean you want to know more about the sentient talking worm? That's through the *right* door to this room. We're dealing with the *left* door now. Maribella and Asteria will get to the right door later, don't worry, and then you'll have all the sentient talking worm you could possibly want.

So anyway, where was I before you interrupted me? Oh

yes, they found a wooden ladder placed right up against the stone wall, leading upward to a trap door.

"My word, how curious," said Maribella. "A ladder. Let's see where it leads."

"I will now go first," announced Asteria, stopping Maribella.

"Why ever so?"

"There could be danger above. I will go in case of this. Then you may follow."

"Oh, well that's awfully nice of you. I can't imagine what sort of danger there could be though."

"A family of rabid garbage bandits."

Maribella was halfway up the ladder before she realized Asteria meant raccoons. There were no raccoons, though. What they discovered was the coziest little reading nook Maribella had ever seen.

It was the third floor tower visible from outside. She had always thought it was just a decorative flourish to the building, as she had never discovered the room before. But now she stood in it, amazed at the find.

The room was very small. Just a few steps across, really. Octagonal in shape, with glass windows surrounding Maribella on every wall. They were above Leafhaven, and had a good view of the entire town. A bear skin rug was spread out on the planks of the floor, and on one side of the room sat an iron fireplace with its iron chimney leading up to the pointed roof of the little tower. In front of the fireplace was a single large, cushioned chair with a matching ottoman.

"A lookout tower?" asked Asteria, circling the room. "For defense against invasion?"

"I think this place was more likely a reading room," said Maribella, testing out the chair. It might have been the most comfortable chair she'd ever sat in, and also the largest. "Probably for the previous owner to come up and get away from everything to read."

It was late in the day, and the sky was overcast with cold,

grey clouds. They rumbled, thunder sounding far away, and the first raindrops of the season began to pelt against the glass. They came slowly, and then in greater number, culminating in a gentle rain shower that enveloped the tiny room in soft noise. The sensation was immediately calming to Maribella. Her muscles relaxed, and a smile came over her face.

"Asteria," she said.

"Yes," said Asteria, nose against a window, watching the water fall on the town.

"A while back, you called me Bell."

Rain filled the silence between them.

"I did," said Asteria finally.

"My name is Maribella, though. Why call me Bell?"

"Bell is part of Maribella, yes? Such is the way names can be made, from another name."

"Well, yes, that can happen, sure. People have nicknames, and well, pet names and the like. Nobody else has ever called me Bell, though."

And here, Asteria bent her head upward so she looked not at the town, but at the dark clouds overhead. "On clear nights, you can see the stars."

Maribella bit at her lip, and followed Asteria's gaze out the window.

"In the Ha-Mazan Tribes, the stars are very important to us."

"Yes, I've heard about that. They're a part of your culture and religion. You believe your spirit will travel to the stars after you die."

"This is true. I do not know what you southerners think of stars, but in the north we found shapes and figures and things in the stars. They tell us a story."

"Yes, we have them too. We call them constellations. We have astronomers who study the stars and name them."

"We have names for the stories in the night sky too. There is one cluster of stars, the brightest and the most beautiful stars in all the darkness, in the shape of a bell. We call it the North

Bell."

Maribella tried to say something, but her heart just then twisted in on itself, and she bit at her finger to hide her mouth.

"You remind me of it," said Asteria, her voice soft. "Whenever I see you, I see those stars."

The rain fell steady, and the outside world went away. There in the little tower of the Cozy Quill Bookshop, the two occupants lived in their own world.

"Asteria..." said Maribella.

"I am not going to stay here forever," said Asteria.

Maribella sat up a little, her eyebrows pushing in on themselves. "What do you mean?"

"I mean I am going to leave soon. Leave this town."

"You can't. I still need you."

"You can run bookshop yourself. This I see. I was not meant for this."

"That's *absurd*. Why you're the one who tore down those boards so we could get in this very room. I certainly couldn't do it."

"Cozy Quill will eventually run out of boarded up mystery rooms. You will not need me much longer."

"Of course I'll need you. There's plenty of things you help me with that I can't do. You can reach the highest shelf. You lift heavy objects. You chop wood. You're the bookshop's guard."

"We now *want* goblins here. There is no more need for me."

"You guard against other things. Like Lady Malicent, for one."

"I cannot stop her if she wanted to destroy this place."

Maribella shook her head and thought some. *This simply isn't like Asteria at all. What's gotten into her?*

"I do not know when I will leave," said the barbarian. "Perhaps after winter."

Maribella got up from the chair and stood by her. "Asteria, talk to me. Tell me what this is really about. I do need you. I'll even up your pay if that's what you want. Why do you want to leave?"

In the grey gloom—the gentle light of rain against the window reflecting onto Asteria's blue eyes—she looked down at Maribella. For a moment, Maribella thought those eyes looked like the stars that Asteria venerated so.

"I know where you really came from," said Asteria.

Maribella brought her hands together in front of herself, but said nothing.

"You never told me," continued Asteria. "You never told anyone. I have paid attention. You always change the subject. But I know where you came from. The northern border towns of Fraey Tarta."

Maribella swallowed.

"You left," said Asteria. "You had to leave. Because my people began their invasion."

Maribella blinked away a growing tear. "I did."

"I am sorry."

"It's not your fault. You didn't do anything."

"And yet I am still melancholy." Asteria left the window and sat on the ottoman, her shoulders slumping, her gaze on the floor. "I have been plagued by melancholy the entire time I have been in Leafhaven. I thought it would leave me eventually. But it has only gotten worse. It is weighing on me. It is causing me great sadness. It is why I must leave."

"But I don't understand," said Maribella, staying at the window. "Why are you so sad? I thought you've been happy here."

"I would be happy here. I would be. If things were normal. If this was my fate."

Maribella paused, caught off guard. "Fate?"

"To the Ha-Mazan Tribes, there is nothing more important than fate. Fate is what dictates everything. It guides our lives. We live according to fate."

"I don't understand."

"Not many southerners would. You have your religions. Your beliefs. We have ours. We believe in fate. And we believe if you go against fate, then your spirit will disappear into nothing after you die. If you follow the path fate has set out for you, then your spirit will travel to the stars after you die. You see, Maribella, I do not want my spirit to disappear. I want to live among the stars after I die."

Maribella of course didn't share these beliefs, and someone with less empathy than her might have gone and made light of Asteria's concern, but not Maribella. She felt the pain in Asteria's heart. "But I still don't fully understand. How are you going against your fate?"

"Our culture is organized by families," said Asteria. "The family you are born into is fated to live a certain way of life. There are merchant families. Farming families. Hunters. Rulers. Warriors. Medicine-makers. There are a great many different families in our many tribes, and each one has a fate tied to it."

Maribella dared to draw closer. "What family were you born into, then? What is your fate?"

Asteria lifted her stare to Maribella. "Helsdottir. My family is a highly respected one. Going back generations, we have had the honor of protecting the ruler of our tribe. We are guardians. Protectors. Warriors with very specific focus. We are destined, every one of us, to protect our queen."

"Protect the queen..."

"The very same queen who has invaded the northern border of little kingdom of Fraey Tarta. The very same queen who is now attacking the lands you have just fled from. It is my fate to live my life protecting her."

"Oh..." Maribella looked down, unsure what to say.

"We are fated to be enemies. I am fated to give my life for my queen. But then, one day, my queen made the decision to invade the southern lands. I could not condone this. It was...evil, to me. And so I fled, much like you fled. But I fled not just from my lands, not just from my responsibility. I fled from my fate. And now, because of my decision, when I die, I will not live on in the stars. I will cease to exist."

Maribella lifted her head to find Asteria's intense gaze.

"Unless I go back. Unless I go back and carry out my fate. Unless I protect my queen."

"But…" said Maribella, shaking her head, her eyes welling with tears.

"I thought I could live this way," said Asteria. "I thought I could accept it. But the melancholy has become too great. I now realize that I cannot. As much as it will pain me to do so, I must embrace my fate again. One day, I will leave here, Bell. One day, I will take my fated place at my queen's side again, and I will devote my life to protecting her. I have made this decision. I am sorry."

Slowly and silently, Maribella sat on the ottoman next to Asteria. Neither woman said anything, but only sat and listened to the rain falling steadily all around them.

Interlude

We have officially come to the halfway point of our story, and so it's time for an interlude.

How are you enjoying the story so far? I hope you're not too sad from that last chapter. It was a bleak one, I know.

Do you think Maribella's bookshop will make it? How will she outwit the wicked Lady Malicent? Where has Baron Blauca disappeared to? Will Dave ever find a girlfriend? Will Gidget just sleep and eat forever? Will Maribella get a happy ending?

But the real question you should be asking is: will *Lady Malicent* get a happy ending?

Now would be a good time to move about and stretch. Perhaps go for a brief walk or roll and see the outside world a bit. Drink some water, maybe have some lunch or dinner if you're hungry. It's not good to do one thing for too long, you know.

All right, then. Are you all finished going about and seeing how boring the real world without a book is? Continue reading, then.

Chapter 16

The Pumpkin Festival Comes to Leafhaven

The days grew colder and rainier. Word from lands close and far away slowly trickled into town. Maribella always kept her ears open for rumors, and rumors she heard aplenty about the recent going ons in Fraey Tarta. The border was still under attack by the Ha-Mazan Tribes, apparently. The King of Fraey Tarta was in a rage, they said, and he was now mustering every able bodied man across his lands to fight. The Queen of Fraey Tarta was also growing sicker by the day, they said, and she hadn't been able to leave her room in weeks.

But Maribella put all that out of her head.

And then eventually the Pumpkin Festival fell on Leafhaven.

Maribella had been spending the day with Clarence the oldest man in town. They were having a nice sit down on the first floor of the Cozy Quill as the rain fell, reading and chatting together. Clarence knew much of the town, and Maribella found she enjoyed talking to him.

"Oh, but the world would be so much better if Lady Malicent wasn't in it," said Maribella, venting to Clarence about the trouble that ever lingered over her head. She didn't like talking about it to Asteria anymore, because Asteria just kept bringing up tables-for-sale and Maribella wanted nothing to do with violence.

"House Malicent," said Clarence, shaking his head and

squinting off into the distance as if trying to remember something. "You know, something unusual about that family comes to mind, now. They've always been a big presence in town, you know, the current Lady as well as her parents before her. But back long ago—oh, I'd say just before the bookshop's original owner died—I remember a manservant of House Malicent coming to the shop every week or so it seemed. Strange, I found that. This must have been a good twenty years ago now, but it just came back to me. Oh well, doesn't matter. Everyone stopped coming after the place closed down back then."

"That doesn't help me now, unfortunately," said Maribella. "If only I could plead my case to Baron Blauca. I feel like Lady Malicent is holding a knife over me without some kind of closure to this whole ordeal."

Maribella and Clarence were then reminded of the Pumpkin Festival when Asteria came bursting in the front door with something in her hands.

"I have found wondrous creation," announced Asteria, holding aloft the object.

Clarence looked up from his massive tome after turning a cracking page. "You found a pie."

Maribella put down her book and got up, giving the pie a good once over. "Hmm, it seems to be of the pumpkin variety. And also half-eaten."

"Pumpkin pie is wondrous creation," said Asteria. "I am much in love with pumpkin pie."

"It certainly is...but oh! That reminds me. It's Pumpkin Festival time, isn't it?"

Clarence looked back down to his book. "It's about that time of the year."

Maribella ran to the front window, ignoring the sleeping Gidget, and looked out to see people dashing about in the rainy street. Down at the market would be plenty of vendors selling pumpkin-themed creations, pies being the most common. "I can't believe I forgot about it. Time does seem to be flying lately."

Asteria reverently placed the pie on the table and joined

Maribella at the window. "Pumpkin...Festival?"

"Yes, that's right."

"What is...Pumpkin...Festival?"

"Well it's a festival of pumpkins, of course. Leafhaven, being a pumpkin town, would naturally have a pumpkin festival. The town grows pumpkins earlier in the year, then harvests them around autumn, but as the season grows old, well, the pumpkins start growing old too. So the town has to use them up, naturally. And that's how the Pumpkin Festival came to be. Did I get all that right, Clarence?"

"That you did," said Clarence, turning a page. "This bookshop always did celebrate Pumpkin Festival back in its day long before you arrived, it did."

"Well then I suppose we should keep the tradition going," said Maribella, turning back to the pie.

"We will now eat remainder of pie, yes?" asked Asteria.

Maribella just now noticed the pie remains on Asteria's fingers. "Uh, yes, but let's do it civilized, shall we? We've got the knives and forks, but the plates seem to be all in the wash. This won't do."

Clarence cleared his throat. "There are plates and bowls in a box on the bottom left drawer of that cabinet behind the front desk."

Maribella paused for a moment, caught of guard, then explored the cabinet. "Well then," she said, discovering a well-stored collection of plates and bowls. "They're here, just as you said they'd be, Clarence." She looked up at him. "How did you know that?"

Clarence was back to reading his book, his face down.

"Clarence?" said Maribella, louder this time.

"Oh, what was that you said?" He tapped his ear.

Maribella shook her head. "Never mind. Here we are. Come along, Asteria, have a plate and a fork. We don't eat pie with our hands."

They ate their fill and then fed the last bits to Gidget. Maribella and Asteria stood and watched early evening grow darker and the rain continue to fall soft and steady. People dashed down the street with umbrellas over their heads and glowing lanterns in their hands.

"The market will be full of pumpkin paraphernalia," said Maribella.

"We must venture to market, then," said Asteria.

"It's so rainy out. I've got a dingy little umbrella for myself, but nothing to cover someone as big as you."

"I will stand in rain."

"Nonsense. You'll catch cold doing that. I won't let you do that for me."

"I do it for pumpkins."

"It wouldn't be comfortable."

"Not everything must be comfortable, Bell. Sometimes, you must do uncomfortable thing."

Maribella fidgeted. *Well, I'm no stranger to uncomfortable ventures*, she thought. *Though you wouldn't know.*

And just then, a tall, thin man wearing a long black coat nearly danced into view before the window. He turned to the two women, revealing a skull masquerade mask that hid the upper half of his face. He smiled at the women and gave a deep, dramatic bow. Townspeople passed him, paying him no attention. He held a long, black pole that reached above his head, and secured at the top of this pole was the top portion of a gargantuan pumpkin's shell, complete with a big stalk pointing upward. Four glowbug lanterns were built into this pumpkin-umbrella, so that plenty of green, almost otherworldly light emanated from the man and his strange tool.

He rose from his deep bow and beckoned the women with a finger.

"I will now destroy this monster," said Asteria without a trace of humor in her voice.

"He's a townsperson, for goodness sake!" said Maribella. "Dressed up for the Pumpkin Festival. And it looks like he's offering that big pumpkin-umbrella to paying customers. Come along, let's try it. It probably won't be too much."

"Hmm," hummed Asteria, following as Maribella pulled her hand.

"We won't be gone long, Clarence, watch the shop for us!"

Clarence grunted and turned another page in his book.

The townsperson seemed even taller close up, almost as tall as Asteria. And the pumpkin-umbrella was mightily impressive. It was like a small, mobile awning made from a giant pumpkin top carted around on a long pole.

"A tour through the town, if you like," said the man, inclining his head and holding his long-fingered hand out. "Only a mere three copper bits, if you like."

"Oh, we like," said Maribella, and produced the bits. "Come on, Asteria. We can see the Pumpkin Festival after all."

Together, pressed close against each other so they both fit under the pumpkin-umbrella, Maribella and Asteria traveled down the street and toward the market. Their guide's lanterns lit up everything in a soft glow. Maribella looked up at the roof of their pumpkin and listened to rain pelting against the rind. She smiled as Asteria followed her gaze in awe.

"Get your pumpkins before they go bad!" called one vendor, and his collection of pumpkins indeed seemed as if they were already going bad. He was a foolish seller, seeing as everyone knows that the Pumpkin Festival is all about the various concoctions and creations you can make with pumpkins, and those are best when the pumpkin is good and matured. And by the time Pumpkin Festival came around, there were no immature pumpkins to be found.

There were the pies, of course. Asteria wanted more of them, but Maribella wisely urged caution. They needed room for the puddings and the pastries and the tea and beer and other drinks all made and mixed with pumpkins. Asteria sampled them all.

"Pumpkin is greatest of all vegetable," she said solemnly.

"They're actually a fruit," said Maribella.

"Pumpkin is greatest of all fruit."

They bought a big bag of roasted pumpkin seeds and

shared them while they toured the town. All of Leafhaven seemed transformed for the festival, as if the town itself had dressed up, just like many of its people. Asteria noticed certain decorations like skulls here and there.

"What do pumpkins have to do with corpses?" she asked.

"There aren't any *corpses* around here," said Maribella. "Those are just decorative skulls. Pumpkin Festival is sort of a Leafhaven specific event, but it incorporates many festivals taking place around this time the world over. It's about the celebration of the passing of things, of recognizing the cycle of nature, of how things grow and mature and then pass on, just like the pumpkins do. Some people take the festival more seriously, and celebrate the lives of those who have come and gone before us. Our ancestors and the like. And...well, anyone else who has passed on."

"I see," said Asteria. "Yes, the Tribes have similar festivals. We do not have pumpkins though."

They stood and watched bands playing and jesters jesting and troupes acting out plays. There were tumblers and singers. And they even found a priestess near a quiet cathedral who offered prayers for those who sought her out.

And through it all, their pumpkin guide followed them silently, holding his pumpkin-umbrella over their heads. They stood without words across from the cathedral, watching the priestess. Asteria seemed awed by the scene.

The rain continued to fall and it grew colder. Maribella drew closer to Asteria, and without giving it more than a cursory thought, she grabbed her hand in her own. Asteria didn't respond other than to give it a little squeeze. It was warm.

For an unfathomable reason that Maribella couldn't explain, her heart twisted in her chest.

One day, I will leave here, Bell.

Asteria's words from the other week echoed in Maribella's head. The words that had twisted her heart just as much as it twisted now. She looked up at her barbarian, and watched her as she watched the priestess. Her face was so solemn, so serious.

Not just yet, you won't leave, thought Maribella. *Not yet.*

She didn't know how long they'd been gone. It almost felt like a dream, really. All she knew was their guide eventually brought them back to the bookshop as the night grew old. A surprised Clarence stood on the covered porch as the women approached and darted under the safety of the awning.

"Wha..." he said, stammering.

"We were just gone to see the festival," said Maribella with a smile. "Just like I said before we left."

"But...Maribella..."

"Yes? What is it?"

"You're both dry as a bone."

"Well of course we are. We had our guide here holding his great pumpkin-umbrella over us the whole time."

"Guide?"

"Yes, him." Maribella turned around and pointed at space filled only with rain.

"But...there's nobody there."

"Oh." Maribella put a finger to her lips. "He must have dashed off."

"Dashed off?" Maribella turned back to Clarence, and his face twisted in both wonder and fear. "Why, Maribella, there was nobody there with you the entire time you walked down the street. You and Asteria were walking under the pouring rain. And now here you stand, dry as a bone!"

"But no, that can't be." Maribella searched the street. "We paid him three bits and everything. We both saw him."

"Three bits?" repeated Clarence, growing whiter than usual. "Tell me, was he a very tall lad? Almost as tall as Asteria here? And was he awfully thin? With a skull mask over his face? And he carried a great pumpkin-umbrella?"

"Yes, exactly that. So you have seen him. What was his name? I hadn't seen anyone else that tall in town before."

Clarence leaned back and shook his head. "Oh, dear lass. That was no townsman. You paid for passage on the Pumpkin Spirit's ride."

Maribella's skin went cold. "But that's—"

"Just a fairy tale?" Clarence leaned in close, one eye narrowing. "Oh, but all fairy tales sprout from a seed of truth. A pumpkin seed, in this case. The great spirit rises for one night every year on this very night. He offers a service for a mere three lowly bits, and those who refuse to pay end up paying with their lives instead. You got lucky, you did, mistaking him for a townsperson and paying his fare. Great luck indeed..."

Clarence walked off, muttering to himself and shaking his face, making several religious gestures with his hand.

Asteria looked up into the rainy night sky. "Falling stars," she said in awe. "A god of pumpkins...we are pumpkin-blessed, Bell."

"Oh, I'm not so sure about that," said Maribella. "More like pumpkin-haunted. And now, well, I'm a bit spooked. Would you mind, if it wasn't too much trouble, making your pallet on my bedroom floor tonight? Just in case of another Pumpkin Spirit visit or the like?"

Asteria nodded her head with determined seriousness. "I will do this thing. I will protect you."

Chapter 17

Maribella and Asteria Read Some More Books

The following two chapters should ideally be read while it's raining or during a thunderstorm. If one isn't readily available, you can wait until weather worsens if you'd like. But if you're the impatient type you could also read them now, even if it's hot and sunny outside where you currently are. You'll just have to use your imagination for the storm.

"It's too cold and rainy outside. Let's stay inside and read some books."

Maribella had made the executive decision to officially try out the little tower reading nook above the second floor. She had cleaned the place up prior to this and placed some pumpkin candles about for light and scent, and stocked the wood supply for the fireplace. She hefted her satchel of chosen books over her shoulder and climbed up the ladder, Asteria close behind.

Upon reaching the room, the women were surrounded by a storm at night. The rain fell heavier than usual, and the town beyond was mostly dark with little dots of solitary lamps shimmering through the storm. The thunder was subdued, but still made its presence known every once in a while with a distant flash and low rumble.

The big chair had a nice, fresh blanket on it, along with a few pillows, and a tray of tea sat next to it. "Here we are," said Maribella.

"But there is only one chair," said Asteria. This was quite

observant of her, for indeed there was only the one chair. "How can we sit and read without second chair?"

"Like this." Maribella hopped onto the chair and patted the space next to her. "You're big, but not *that* big. Come on, we can both fit."

"Hmm," murmured Asteria, smoothly nodding her head. "I will now do this thing you ask."

And soon the two were snugly secured under their thick fur blanket surrounded by a rainstorm. The fire crackled cheerily, and it was quite warm. Not just from the fire, but from sitting right next to Asteria. Maribella smiled.

"I do not understand," said Asteria as she looked about.

"What don't you understand?"

"Why move all the way up here just to read? What was wrong with spot by the fireplace on first floor?"

"Because this was built as a reading nook."

"Was something wrong with first floor place?"

"No. It was a perfectly fine place to read. But this is a better place."

"Why?"

"Because look around. Sometimes the environment and atmosphere of where you're reading has an effect on the enjoyment of reading."

"Oh? Tell me of this dark magic."

"It's not magic. It's just how it works."

"I do not understand."

"Well..." Maribella bit her bottom lip, looking out at the storm and then to the crackling fire. "Just look around. Here we are, up in a tiny room all alone, but also completely surrounded by cold, wet, harsh elements. But we're not out in those elements. We're safe and secure, tucked away under a blanket, and very comfortable. We have tea, a fire, these lovely candles. And each one of those lamps out there in town is its story. But we're not down there, we're right here in our own story. It's...well, it's cozy is what I'm trying to say."

"Hmm."

"And that's the best way to enjoy a book. When you're cozy. Does that make sense?"

Asteria sagely nodded, narrowing her eyes and looking off into the distance. "The windows showing storm reminds us the existence of danger nearby, but we are safe from danger, and do not have to concern ourselves with it, thus allowing us to focus more on reading task at hand. And so we are both reminded of the threat, yet calmed by its taming, and thus we experience pleasure."

"Uh, well, that...might be surprisingly accurate? I don't know why it is. It just is. But come now, here we are, I brought several books that might be interesting."

They flipped through a few offerings. Asteria took a rather large book in her hands and sighed forlornly. For a moment she sounded like Dave the forlorn doorman.

"What's the matter?" asked Maribella. "Would you rather do something else?"

"No, I am happy doing this. It is only, I am so slow a reader. I must sound out every word before going on. And yet there are so many books, and so many of them are so very large."

"It doesn't matter how fast a reader you are. As long as you enjoy doing it, that's all that matters."

"But you are so very fast a reader. I will never catch up."

"And that's why I'm reading for you. Here we are."

They looked at a few books, and one was a collection of grim poetry that generally was a delight and fit the current mood in that little nook quite nicely. Asteria seemed to enjoy poetry, but also grew weary of it rather quickly, so Maribella moved on. They also spent some time on a short story about a murder and investigation that Asteria quite enjoyed, but Maribella found a bit morbid. It was a well-written story, but unfortunately it was written by a bitter rival of yours truly, so I won't mention it or its author's name, and I feel absolutely no guilt for this decision whatsoever.

"Ah, here we are," said Maribella, picking up a short novel and dusting off its dirty and stained cover. "*The Adventures of*

Lily Lovelace. I've never heard of it, but this sounds like it could be up your alley."

The novel started out simply enough. The protagonist was a young woman who worked at a flower shop—worked at, didn't own—and she was treated rather poorly by her employer. There was plenty of pathos created for her and the author did well at making you care about our poor heroine. It didn't take long, however, for Asteria to stop the proceedings.

"Why is this sounding so very different from other books?" she asked.

"Ah," said Maribella. "I'm glad you noticed. Both the point of view and the tense of this book are different than the norm. Most books are written in third person point of view and in past tense. This one is written in first person point of view and in present tense."

"None of these words you say make sense. You are toying with me now."

"No, it's true! See, it's told from Lily's point of view, as if she's sitting here talking to us, and it's also told as if it's happening right now this very moment."

"I see. This is good."

They continued reading. It didn't take long for Lily Lovelace to be captured by a band of outlaws and ridden out to the woods to the outlaw's camp. Maribella surmised this was the "adventure" part of the book referenced in the title.

It wasn't until a couple chapters in that things began to get strange.

To my surprise, the outlaws don't bother tying me up. The idea of escape crosses my mind. But there are so many brutes milling about the camp that it seems impossible. Do I even know where I am? Can I even find my way back home?

Oh, how I long for the simple life of a flower shop girl now.

The bandits are all tall and rugged, and they don't seem overly cruel. They watch me with predatory eyes, and some of them smile at me. As eve falls and the air grows cold, I look into the darkness to plot my escape.

"You don't want to try running," says one of the brutes. My heart flashes in my chest at his hungry gaze. "We'll just have to chase you down again. Ah hah!"

His fellows laugh, and I very much feel like the butt of a joke. As fires are lit, a man arrives in camp who I can only assume is their leader. He is the tallest of them all, with the broadest of shoulders, and the squarest of jaws with the most rugged of stubble on said jaw. He saunters into the camp, and the men salute and cheer him.

He approaches me and I recoil in fear. He doesn't attack, though. He places a boot on a rock and rests his elbow on his knee, and looks me up and down as if I were some won prize.

"You have nothing to fear from me, my lady," he says, his eyes glinting in the night.

"I'm but a humble flower shop girl," I say. "You have mistaken me for a noble of some kind. There is nobody with any money to pay my ransom. Please, let me go."

"I am he who called for your capture, but it 'twasn't on account of a ransom."

"It 'twasn't?"

"Nay. You may be confused now, but allow me to explain who I am."

"I know who you are. You're an outlaw."

"Yes, I am an outlaw. The leader of this gang of outlaws. But I am so very more than that."

"What do you mean?"

"Tell me, Lily, have you ever heard of a millionaire?"

"Yes."

"Do you know what a millionaire is?"

"Of course. It's someone with a lot of money, like a noble or a king. They have millions of doubloons."

"Well, Lily, I must tell you that I am not a millionaire."

"Oh."

"I'm a billionaire.*"*

I breastily gasp, swooning, fighting to stay awake. I know I must make my escape soon, even though my captor is a six foot five inch billionaire outlaw leader.

"Lily, take my hand," he undulates.

I follow his command, uncertain and afraid...yet thrilled. I am tamed by his aura.

"That is not all there is to tell," he says.

Behind him I see men still, but mixed among them are wolves pacing about. "Wolves!" I ejaculate, pointing behind him.

"Lily," he says, and his eyes begin to glow. "I am not just an outlaw. I am not just a billionaire. I am also the alpha of my pack. We are half-men, half-wolves." His shirt opens as the moon rises in fullness, and he pectorals his way closer to me. His eyes turn yellow. "And I have smelled your scent. This is why I ordered your capture. You are to be my mate, Lily. Do not deny it. I can smell your

"Nope!" said Maribella, slamming the book shut.

"We were just getting to the good part!" said Asteria, unusually animated.

"Just what is this we're reading?" Maribella looked at the front cover again. It was covered in dust still, and she used her elbow to clean it up, revealing the true full title hidden under dirt, complete with a subtitle at the bottom. "Oh!" she cried upon realization.

The Lusty Adventures of Lily Lovelace

An Outlaw, Billionaire, Shifter Romance

"This is definitely not something we're reading," said Maribella.

"I like outlaw billionaire shifter romances," said Asteria.

"We'll have to create a restricted collection in one of these small side rooms I suppose, where we can store all the scandalous books." Maribella moved to put the book on the stack, but Asteria reached for it.

"Keep reading," said Asteria, laughing as Maribella clambered away. "I want to know what happens to Lily."

Maribella tried to not laugh and ended up snorting as she

held the book far out from the chair. "No indeed! She very well should have stayed back in her flower shop if she knew what was good for her."

Asteria continued laughing, loud and hearty. It was a rare sound to hear, and Maribella realized she enjoyed hearing it. "But what of life with outlaw, billionaire, wolf-man? Will she be his mate?"

Maribella tossed the book and it slid across the floor, safely away from Asteria's grasp. The two women laughed together for a moment, reveling in the absurdity of the tale they were just in, and before either one knew it Maribella had leaned right up against Asteria's side in the chair, and the two sat there, looking into the fire together and gathering themselves after the hardy laugh. Maribella's head rested right against Asteria's arm.

Maribella wanted to stay there forever.

But she sat upright again and blushed. "Sorry."

Asteria seemed genuinely confused. "For what?"

"Here. We can't end the night with Lily Lovelace. How about one more reading before going to bed? This one is a short story from a collection. I read it once a long while ago."

"Why call this a short story? It seems so long."

"Oh, it's only a couple thousand words."

"A couple thousand!"

"It's not all long as that, trust me. And it reads very fast, once you get into it. It's pretty much just a conversation between two people, and showcases how something as simple as that can be full of tension and conflict and mystery. I brought it up here tonight because I felt like it fit perfectly with the thunderstorm outside. The author is unknown, and the story is called *Encounter on the Eastern Sea*."

Chapter 18

Encounter on the Eastern Sea

The storm rumbled in every direction for leagues, and rain fell in gentle sheets. Dozens of dark waterspouts spun on the horizon, threatening to circle in on the lonely little boat at sea.

She only had a single lantern to guide her. Its dim light shone before her skiff, cutting through the drizzle. Evening came quick, and the sea took on an otherworldly air.

Another light emerged from the darkness. She peered through the rain, squinting. It was a boat, slightly larger than her own. All along its sides were bright colors, painted designs. There were several hanging lanterns casting orange and red onto its wooden deck, bobbing as the boat drifted forward.

She grabbed her oar and paddled to intercept it, securing both vessels together with a rope when they bumped into each other. There didn't initially seem to be anyone aboard the other boat, but a yellow light glowed behind a curtain leading into a small, short cabin.

Sticking her head inside, she was met with welcoming warmth and candlelight. The cabin was filled with aromas: herbs, flamed fish, pungent wine. Her mouth watered as she shook her wet hair and pulled it back behind her ears.

"So," came a crackly old voice, "I'm not the only fool drifting out here in the middle of nowhere, eh?"

There he sat, cross-legged, at the cabin's rear. The ceiling was too low to stand properly, and she had to duck down onto her knees to go inside. She crouched at the entrance, feeling raindrops patter down her back.

"No," she agreed. "I guess you're not."

"What's your name, lass?"

"What's yours?"

His attention was directed toward a short table. He had his little meal there: roasted fish on a plate, a jug of wine, two cups. There was also incense burning, filling the cabin with a pleasant smell.

"Oh, I'm afraid I've forgotten mine," he said and he took a deep whiff of his dinner.

"You've forgotten your name?"

"Aye. It's not that hard when you're out here by yourself for long enough."

"And why exactly are you out here to begin with? It's a strange place for a hermit, yes?"

"Who said I'm a hermit?" he asked, finally looking up. "Why are you sitting all the way over there? Come closer, girl, by the light here."

"I'd prefer to stay where I am. That is, until I know just who you are."

"So rude," he said. "You come onto my boat, uninvited, and demand to know about *me*? What about you, girl? What are you doing in the middle of the eastern sea, the most forsaken watery domain in the world?"

"I'm a traveling merchant."

"Hmm," said the old man, scratching his whiskers. "All right then. Myself? Why, you guessed rightly. I'm just a hermit, and the ocean is my solitude. Now, girl, please come closer."

She moved, crawling several feet farther into the cabin. Some rainwater dripped from cracks in the ceiling above, but it was still more comfortable than her skiff would have been.

"Now me? I can brave these waters," the old man continued talking. "I live on them. But you, young girl, have a landlubber's look about you. Do you know what dwells in the eastern sea?"

"What would that be?"

"All sorts of oddities not of this world. To begin with, do you believe those waterspouts out there ever subside? Nay, they're eternal. And have you not heard about the man-eating monster of the eastern sea? It takes its victims in its massive mouth, filled with sharp teeth, and drags them to the seabed to feast on. And what about the ghost ship? A pirate ship, they say, that only appears on these waters when the moon is full. It passes in the night, its skeletal crew looking overboard at those below, and if you stare too long, then you'll join them, a phantom crewmember. And of course don't forget my favorite, the banshee. She wails on the horizon, threatening to overtake weary men on weary ships, screaming with a ghostly corpse's voice. She's the worst! My hair stands on end just thinking about her!"

His old eyes had gone wide with fear.

"Yes. I know about those things," the woman said. "But these oddities must not actually exist if you've been sailing here for so long and you're still alive."

He hunkered lower over his steaming fish. "Oh, they exist. I've seen them. I've seen the great whirlpool that never sleeps and sucks down ships. I've seen the monster of the eastern sea lure boats to what looks like land, only to wreck them with a giant fin. The ghost ship has scraped my own boat, and my hull has the marks to prove it. And of course, I've heard the wail of the sea banshee, late at night, while sleeping here on my pallet. But I'm at one with the ocean, and it does no harm to me. Visitors, well, that's another story."

The two sat, listening to the timbers creak. The wind sounded vaguely like a woman weeping.

"So, lady merchant, who are you really? That skiff you have is too small for business. And besides, what trading could you possibly do out here?"

She smiled. "I'm a pirate, come to loot any ships I come across."

"Ah," sighed the man.

"And who are you, really?"

"Well then! You don't believe an old man like myself could live out here alone? I suppose you're right about that. I'm a fisherman, not just a simple hermit. I go wherever it's best to make the biggest catch. Now, why not sit closer?"

She crawled halfway into the cabin. "Not afraid of me after learning I'm a pirate?"

"I have nothing worth taking. Nothing but fish, which I share freely. Why not have some?"

"For now, I think I'll pass."

She sat cross-legged, like the old man, and watched him as he poured a cup of wine.

"Nothing like the grapes to warm a body on a night like this," he said, drinking some down. The water leaking from the ceiling began to drip more quickly. She blinked her eyes, detecting a salt sting in the droplets.

"Isn't it a bit far out to be fishing?" she asked.

"Aye, aye. Isn't it a bit far out to be pirating?"

"Yes," she said, keeping her eyes fixed on his. "About this banshee, what do you think she wants? Why does she wail?"

"What do all banshees want? I haven't a clue, though I know enough to stay out of their way. You wouldn't happen to be one, would you? Or better yet, you might be… yes, a siren! Here to lure me into your deadly claws!"

Her smile broadened, showing her bright white teeth. "Maybe I am."

"You could definitely pass for one, with a face like that."

"You think I would admit if I were one?"

"Aye, you have a point. I suppose there's no tellin'."

She lifted a leg, wrapping her hands around her knee. "There's one way," she said. "How about this? How about I tell you who I *really* am, and you tell me who you *really* are?"

"Who you really are, and who I really am?"

"No lying this time. We both swear it."

"The truth?" The old man put down his cup and thought

a moment. "Aye. The truth this time. And we swear it. All right then, who are you?"

She looked gravely at him. "I'm a siren. You guessed it."

He paused a moment, rubbed his fingers through his whiskers again. "Hmm. And you plan on doing me in? For dinner, maybe?"

"Maybe," she said, and shrugged.

"Maybe," he repeated, and then he gave a short laugh. "Ha! Or maybe not. Now you'll be wantin' to know who I really am, aye?"

"I would."

"Well, lady siren, you may wonder how I know these waters so well—all about the monster of the eastern sea, and the banshee? I'll tell you, and you'll see why I don't fear any siren. Sit straight and stay sharp, lass, 'cause you're speakin' to a dead man. I'm a ghost, and I'm the banshee's husband at that."

"Is that so?"

"Aye. The dead sail these waters. And that's why the banshee's angry. You see, she's after me. I've been runnin' from her for over fifty years."

"She misses you sorely, I assume."

"Best be careful. I'm a kind specter, but if *she* finds us out, she's liable to freeze your heart with fear, siren or no."

"Oh, I'm being very careful."

"Good. And now that the introductions are over, how about you share a drink with me?"

"Share a drink with a ghost? I'd never pass up the opportunity."

And so she crawled closer, sitting right in front of the old man and his table. The sweet incense faded, and the dripping above grew even more profuse, although the rain had not gotten any heavier.

"Here we are," said the old man. "One cup of wine."

He gave her a cup, and she took it and drank deeply.

"You know," she said, "I've been thinking about all these legends. About the monster of the eastern sea in particular.

People have been hunting it for years, but none have been successful. Do you happen to know why?"

He looked at her, his expression blank.

"That's odd," she continued. "Being a ghost of these waters, I thought you knew everything there was to know. Anyway, they say that it's so difficult to catch because it has... well, strange powers. The ability to create illusions, for instance."

The old man's face was deep in his cup.

"Do you want to know who I *really* am?" she asked.

"Who are you?" whispered the old man, and the boat began to rock.

"I'm a vagabond, a rogue, a thief who will do anything for work, including hunting down a sea monster. In the port city I sailed from, they're holding a contest. Whoever comes back with the tongue of the monster of the eastern sea will earn great riches. Many set out. I plan on winning."

At that, the old man threw his cup aside. "You fork-tongued—"

"Do you know how I can tell?" she asked.

"What went wrong? Am I not the very image of a human being? Is not every detail of myself and this boat lifelike?"

"Oh, it is," she said, setting her own cup down. "But your wine. It's not wine at all. It's seawater."

With that, she lunged, her hand slashing forward from behind her back, carrying with it a blade. It sank into the old man, who wasn't an old man at all. His visage morphed, suddenly jelly-like and wet. She reared back and gave him another hack, until the blob that used to be the old man fell to the floorboards, writhing.

Quickly, she lifted it and turned around. Saliva cascaded from the ceiling, which, again, wasn't what it had seemed. Large teeth cracked and jutted from the wooden walls. Behind her, where the old man had been sitting, a great black hole opened, gaping, a low groan rumbling from its tunnel. The entire structure began to tilt upward, backward, as the thief jumped from the sinking boat, which was not a boat, before it slid down underneath the dark waves.

She splashed and swam for her own skiff, hauling herself aboard, throwing down the fleshy blob, and cutting loose the rope that bound her vessel to the sinking thing. Finally the cord snapped, and she lay back, panting heavily.

She looked down at her prize. She had done it. She had cut out the tongue of the monster of the eastern sea.

Now, standing at the portside wharf before a gathered crowd a few days later, she had her trophy hanging from a winch above the dock, just as a captured shark might have been displayed. But it was not a shark. Curious spectators were staring, and a few children wanted to poke it with their fingers.

"Then do you mean to tell us," demanded one port official, "that this is truthfully the monster's tongue?"

They were all gazing eagerly a her.

"Of course," she said. "That's what I just explained. What reason would you ever have to doubt me?"

"Hmm," pondered Asteria after the story ended. "Very wily, this woman."

"Yes," said Maribella. "I thought you might like this one, since it has a monster in it, and a lady who apparently likes knives and other sharp objects."

"Yes, this is true. But...I am now troubled."

"Over what?"

"It is true that I am not good reader, but I have seen something very curious here. There, near the end of story. I read along with you as you read aloud, and there I see a word written different than what you said. Do you see here? It says, 'They were all gazing eagerly *a* her.' But you said, 'They were all gazing eagerly *at* her.'"

"Ah. That's what we call a *typo*."

"A typo?"

"Yes. Short for a typographical error. A typo is when the author of a story makes a mistake and accidentally misspells a word or uses the wrong word instead of the right one."

"I see. I have found a typo."

"Yes, you did."

"So the author was a poor author?"

"Well, no. If you enjoyed the story, they were a good author."

"But they made a mistake."

"A small one. And besides, I once heard a very wise man say something profound about typos in stories. He said that if a story was ever written completely perfectly without a single error, then it would come to life and jump out of the page. So in order to keep all those horrible dangers found inside books away from the real world, authors always make sure to include at least a single typo in the story so that it doesn't happen. Perhaps this author was simply doing this?"

"Hmm. This magic sounds unlikely, but I will accept it."

Maribella was completely correct here. If there ever was a book, short story, or any kind of fiction without at least one typo contained within, then the characters and the monsters would jump out of the page at you. That would be horrible! And so if you find any typos in this very book you currently hold in your hands, you can rest easy knowing they were put there on purpose, and they weren't an accident on the part of yours truly.

Chapter 19

The Bookshop Has a Bookworm

It is at this point in the story that I must inform the beloved reader (that's you) that the next two chapters will contain two different non-human species. So far we've already had an appearance of one non-human character, that delight of a goblin girl named Gidget (who at this very moment was still sleeping on her display table and being randomly fed by various townspeople). I feel the need to deliver this advance warning because in my experience I've found that humans tend to react rather shocked whenever a fellow or madam of a different species suddenly shows up in front of them. This is an absurd reaction, because of course the world contains all manner of intelligent species who can talk and carry on just fine in daily human society.

Maribella blinked and covered her eyes as splinters flew from the doorway. "Yes," she murmured to herself. "That's it, smash it to bits."

Asteria was putting on quite the display as she reared her battleaxe back and sent it crunching into the locked door over and over again. This door was the one to the right of the door that led to the tower reading nook. Maribella had never found a key for it, and so she finally decided to have Asteria destroy it with her axe, which Asteria was glad to do.

Before continuing on, first we'll have another pop quiz. You didn't forget that this was an interactive story, did you? Well it's too late now. If you didn't run away during the first quiz, then you can't very well go and do so now.

The question you must now answer:

What should you feed ducks?

A) Bread

B) Oats

C) Strawberry Jam

Well? Take your time. This is a tough one. I'll give you a hint. It's not strawberry jam. If you selected that, put this book down and go visit your mother. So is it bread or oats?

The correct answer is none of the above; you shouldn't feed ducks. This was another trick question. You should feed ducks nothing.

Coincidentally, nothing is exactly what Maribella and Asteria found within the locked room. No furniture, no beds, no dressers. But then they looked down. There were dozens upon dozens of books all lying on the floor and opened up.

"How curious," said Maribella, carefully stepping over the books. "It almost looks as if someone purposefully spread out all of these books and opened them."

"This is strange thing to do," said Asteria.

Maribella wrinkled her nose, noticing something else odd about the books. "Look. Some of them are opened to the first page of the book, while others are on the last page, and nothing between. How unusual."

"This is unusual."

The single window to the room was dirty and very little light came through, so it was difficult to see. The women continued to explore, side by side, searching for some kind of clue that would reveal the purpose of this room.

Maribella then spotted something that shocked her so much she sprang into the air and jumped into Asteria's arms.

To Asteria's credit, she simply stood there stoically and dutifully held a trembling Maribella.

"Oh," said Maribella, feeling very foolish when she realized it was just a worm on the page of an open book. Asteria placed her back down and she smoothed her clothing, her face turning only a light shade of red. "It's just a worm."

"This worm is reading book?" said Asteria, stooping down.

The worm looked up. He wore a tiny pair of glasses that were very thick (in relation to the worm's size, of course). His two black eyes were enormous through the magnification.

And then he spoke.

"Aye, that's right mate, I'm readin' this here book, I am."

Maribella and Asteria looked at each other without a word.

Maribella turned back to the worm. "You...can talk?"

The worm's mouth fell into an offended, wide, gaping circle, and his big eyes looked from woman to woman.

The women looked at each other, then to the worm, then back to each other, then the worm again.

"You wot?" said the worm.

"Oh, apologies," said Maribella. "It's just we've never met a talking worm."

"I'm a readin' worm is what I am, 'till you two blokes came along and interrupted, you did."

"You can read?"

"Course I can. I'm a bookworm. It's what we do. We're born, we are, then we go and wiggle our way to the closest book and start readin' it, we do."

Maribella blinked. "How long have you been in this room reading?"

"Oh, years and years, I reckon."

Maribella looked around the room at a loss. "You're telling me you read all these books?"

"Not all of 'em, no. A whole lot of 'em, though. I'm getting there. Slow and steady does it, me mum always used to say, she did."

"But how have you stayed alive all this time?" A horrible thought came into Maribella's head. "Do you eat the pages?"

Once again, the three individuals in the room simply took

turns looking from one to another. The worm's mouth gaped open.

"You wot? You havin' a go at me?"

Maribella cleared her throat. "Sorry, I'm just wondering what you eat. I mean, there is no food in here."

The worm looked to Asteria. "Did this bird fall out of her nest as a chick?" he asked. "Course I don't eat books. I read them. I can't very well read books if I went and ate them, could I?"

"Then what do you eat?"

"What else? I eat dust, of course." And here the bookworm demonstrated, placing his long tongue onto the surface of the page he stood on and then wiggled an inch forward before stopping and smacking his lips. "Ah, this one's a ripe one, it is."

"Oh," said Maribella, unsure how to even react to the display. She looked around the room to see that indeed, there was very little dust about, because the worm had apparently kept it clean all this time.

He had licked the whole place!

Ever so slowly, Asteria leaned down and whispered into her ear. "Do you wish me to destroy this creature?"

"*No*," whispered Maribella, glaring up at Asteria.

The bookworm was already back to reading. Maribella watched him for a bit. He was almost as small as a single word on the page, and she found it fascinating how he slowly crept forward, both eyes focused on a single word as he moved.

Maribella knelt down to get closer to the bookworm. "Excuse me, mister bookworm—"

"You wot?" said the bookworm, snapping up at Maribella with another shocked expression. "I've a name, you know. It's Mr Reginald Cumberbutton. I'm quite a big name in the bookworm world, I'll have you know. How'd you like it if I went and called you miss human? That don't feel too great, now do it?"

"I'm deeply sorry, Mr Cumberbutton. I'm Maribella Waters and this is my friend Asteria Helsdottir. I was just curious how you're able to read all these books, what with you being so very small and slow and all."

"You wot?"

"It's just, the books are so very large, and you're so very small. I didn't mean to be rude or insult you."

"Oh, no worries, love. I s'pose I am a mite slow compared to you giant lot. Well then Ms Waters, I start by wiggling my way over to a book, and then I read the first letter, and then the next letter, and then the one after that. Pretty soon I've got a whole word, I do! And then eventually that word turns into a sentence, and then a paragraph, and then a page. After that, I crawl under the page, crawl back—thereby flipping said page—then I start all over again until I'm done. Bob's your uncle."

"I see. And how long does it take you to finish a whole book, on average?"

"Oh, months and months and months, I'd say. Still, wouldn't trade it for the world. I'm a lil' bookworm, after all, and the world is so very big."

"Who is Bob?" asked Asteria.

"Fascinating," said Maribella. "You've really read many books this way?"

"I have no uncle named so," said Asteria.

"Why I certainly have," said the worm. "Here, I'll demonstrate for you." His thick glasses looked down to the page and his myriads of tiny feet began to move. He didn't inch forward. He millimetered forward.

"T!" he cried out. "Oh, a T. That could turn into anything. Always a good beginning with T. Let's see. And then we have an H. A solid letter, always did like the sound of it. Very soft and smooth. And oh! Here comes the last letter already it seems! This one is a short word, he is. And it's an E. That makes a the! Oh, the. An amazing word it is. It's a portent of things to come. The what? The apple? The tree? The inevitable end of the cosmos and all life as we know it? The what? I'm on the edge of my seat, I am."

He began to hum happily to himself while crawling and reading.

Maribella stood up and the two women just watched the worm slowly read.

"Well then," said Maribella at long last. "I suppose we should leave our bookworm to himself. We'll have to remember to bring Mr Cumberbutton some new books every once in a while."

"Hmm," pondered Asteria, crossing her arms and observing the bookworm. "I am happy we have discovered Mr Cumberbutton."

"Oh? Why so?"

"Because I now know I am not slow reader. I am very fast reader."

Maribella smiled. "I suppose so. Look at him go. It doesn't matter that it takes him longer than most other people to get through a book. He still enjoys them well enough."

"Yes, he does." Asteria nodded solemnly. "This is good."

Chapter 20

The Greatest Person To Have Ever
Lived Visits The Bookshop

T he days rolled by at a leisurely pace, and the town grew
sleepier as winter arrived. With winter came snow,
falling light and timid at first. The sunlight became shier,
and the moon braver and bolder, coming out earlier and casting
its silver glow across Leafhaven's snow-tipped landscapes.

And with the snow came Sir Edmundus Gloopinbottom.
He was the greatest person to have ever lived.

He entered the Cozy Quill Bookshop one day to find
Maribella and Asteria lying about. One of them was reading and
one of them was sharpening an axe (I'll let you guess which did
which). But then the door crashed open and a wave of winter
flurries danced inside, followed by the wonderful Sir Edmundus
Gloopinbottom. A crowd of poor homeless orphans who had
nowhere to go and nothing to eat came in after him.

"Here you are, children," said Sir Edmundus
Gloopinbottom as he handed out coins to the helpless
children. "A handful for everyone, that's right." Sir Edmundus
Gloopinbottom's voice was like that of a baritone angel's. "And I
have food as well. Here we are, sandwiches for all." He passed out
several sandwiches.

"We love you, Sir Edmundus Gloopinbottom," said the
children, whose lives were permanently changed for the better
after meeting their incredible benefactor.

"Oh!" cried Maribella, getting up from her desk. "It's Sir Edmundus Gloopinbottom! Come to visit our workshop! Asteria, look who it is!"

"It is Sir Edmundus Gloopinbottom!" shouted Asteria in amazement. Even Ha-Mazan warriors knew of him.

If you're wondering who Sir Edmundus Gloopinbottom is, you must have lived under a rock your entire life. For everyone knows the amazing author and all of his varied masterworks, his topics ranging from genre fiction to educational texts and everything in between. His real life adventuring is inspiration for many of his releases. He was knighted by Queen Zenobia of the Southern Reaches. He is a writer of unparalleled skill and class. He is the most humble individual in all the world. He is a green slime.

Have you never met a green slime? Oh, what a poor soul you are! Green slimes are some of the most delightful characters you will ever come across. Not to be confused with blue slimes, who are wild, mindless blobs of goop that roam the countryside and are hunted by inexperienced adventurers for experience. No, green slimes are highly intelligent and well-mannered and fine-smelling, and are quite fond of pipes and tea and fashion.

The sparse amount of people inside the bookshop attempted to swarm Sir Edmundus Gloopinbottom, but he would have none of it. "I cannot spend time giving into the endless demands of my legion of fans," he announced, and Maribella and Asteria grew very sad. "For I am conducting research for my current project!" The women's faces lit up again. "I am working on an educational text that will gather all available knowledge of cheeses and compile this knowledge into one all-encompassing guide. It will be called *Sir Edmundus Gloopinbottom's Definitive Guide to Cheese and Cheese Pairings— From the Perspective of a Cultured Slime*."

"Fascinating," said Maribella, watching as the green slime (who was also quite physically striking) made his way down aisles of books with the inhuman speed that only a green slime can muster. He scanned titles and flipped pages with his slime tendrils, taking whatever shape was needed to accomplish the incredible physical feat of combing the entire bookshop. His fans followed him.

Another poor orphan child came out of nowhere and stood in front of Sir Edmundus Gloopinbottom, her lip trembling and snot running down her nose.

"Whatever seems to be the matter, lost child? Did you not receive my alms of coin and food?"

"I did," said the child, her voice so very small. "But I am sick."

"Worry not, child, for I am Sir Edmundus Gloopinbottom." He placed his gloopy tendril onto the orphan's head, and she instantly became healthy again.

With a smile and a hop in her step, she said, "Thanks Sir Edmundus Gloopinbottom! I love you!"

"Think nothing of it!" cried Sir Edmundus Gloopinbottom, going back to tearing through the available selection of books, leaving a wreck in his wake.

You might be slightly confused at this point. Sir Edmundus Gloopinbottom could solve any problem, you see, which is how he healed the sick girl, because he is simply that great. If you're wondering, "Why didn't Sir Edmundus Gloopinbottom help Maribella and Asteria out with their Lady Malicent problem?" then stop asking questions.

Finally, Sir Edmundus Gloopinbottom gathered all the books he needed for his current work-in-progress, and he paid Maribella for them at the front desk, and then gave her even more money simply because he was that generous of a person.

"Thank you for visiting my shop, Sir Edmundus Gloopinbottom," said Maribella. "I'll never forget it. You've changed our lives."

"Think nothing of it," said Sir Edmundus Gloopinbottom.

This next part here is actually true.

"And by the by, I'll be in town for a bit," he continued.

"Oh? That's good to hear."

"Truth be told, I'm actually finishing up my current

project, and I'm thinking I'll be needing to work on something totally different after this. A true biography or story, I'm thinking. That's what my gelatinous soul is telling me I need to write. The only problem is, I have no inspiration!"

"Well that's sad to hear."

"Yes, indeed. But like I said, I'll be about town. This was always a curious little dot on the map, I thought. Perhaps I'll find some townsperson with an interesting story, and I can put their story to paper."

"That would be lovely for the town," said Maribella. "I don't know of anybody offhand, but if I think of someone with a good story, I'll certainly let you know. Goodbye Sir Edmundus Gloopinbottom!"

Chapter 21

Leafhaven Celebrates the Winter Solstice

Get comfortable and brace yourself. This is the Winter Solstice celebration to end all Winter Solstice celebrations, and it's a long one.

Winter grew older and colder as the weeks went by. The days were short, and the nights were long. Dark clouds always seemed to be overhead, full of snow that blanketed the sleepy town of Leafhaven. The harvests were long collected, the stocks of game were salted and stored, the supplies of firewood were piled up high. The work of the year had been done, and now, in the deepness of winter, the people of Leafhaven grew content and happy and warm inside their little houses with crackling fires, surrounded by good friends and family.

Later on in Maribella's life, she would look back at this time and recognize it as possibly the happiest time of her life. She had done what she had set out to do. The bookshop was hers, and it was certified as a complete success in town. The Cozy Quill had become a well-traveled staple. Maribella and Asteria themselves had become beloved characters for the people of Leafhaven. Customers stopped by not just to shop, but to chat and drink tea and even have a nice lunch at the bookshop. It became a place to hide out for a few minutes, and was well-loved.

And for Maribella, this time of her life was new and exciting and wonderful. That winter. That wistful winter that she would look back on for years and feel a deep sense of longing nostalgia over. Have you ever felt that in your life? Perhaps a time during childhood, or when first setting out on your own? It can be a magical period of life no matter what it is, and for Maribella, this magical period was her first winter in Leafhaven. She would look back on it and feel something that almost resembled sadness because she could never travel back and experience it again, but also great happiness because it happened and would always be with her in her memories. It was a wistful nostalgia, one you or I specifically do not share because we have our own, but it's one we can still somehow feel even though we didn't live it.

Asteria was there with her. She hadn't mentioned leaving Leafhaven recently, so that worry had faded away. Even Lady Malicent hadn't shown up again. The women simply ran the shop together, side by side, and kept each other company. The snow piled on the streets, and the world became a very slow, calm and peaceful place, and Maribella was more content than she had ever been in her life.

One day, she was putting up colored glowbug lantern decorations inside the Cozy Quill with Asteria's help.

"What is this Winter Solstice you speak of?" asked Asteria, looking at all the festive lantern screens that would turn the glowbugs' natural green light into reds and blues and oranges.

"It's the very middle of winter," said Maribella. "It's the point when the day is the shortest it'll be all year, and the night is the longest. After tonight we get closer and closer to spring."

"A very cold night this will be."

"That's true, but it's also a time of celebration for us southerners."

"So many festivals you have. What is this one about? Mysterious Goddess of Snow?"

"Not quite. It's a time of enjoying the fruits of the year. We feast, and we spend time with loved ones, and we appreciate life. If the Pumpkin Festival is about celebrating the lives of those who came before, then the Winter Solstice is about celebrating the loved ones we currently have with us."

"I see," said Asteria, her focus on a lantern. "So I would be celebrating you," she added, almost as if an afterthought.

For a long while, Maribella couldn't say anything. She just silently continued to work.

"So," she said at length. "We need the place nice and decorated for the party tonight. I never thought so many people would want to spend Winter Solstice here with us, but well, here we are. One big happy family."

The first person to arrive was Clarence the oldest man in town. He had a short walk, since he lived in the flower shop just a few buildings down the street.

"Am I early?" he asked, leaning on his canes and shuffling toward one of the tables.

"You're right on time," said Maribella with a smile. She was lying. Clarence was very early. She didn't mind, though. She continued preparing everything and chatting when the twins arrived, Captain Hargle and Captain Bargle.

"The most important men of this year's Winter Solstice, coming through!" shouted Hargle. They each carried the end of a big platter with a cooked ham on it. Maribella's eyes grew wide as they placed the platter on a table, and she was transported back in time to her trip to Leafhaven on the back of Edgar the pig farmer's wagon full of pigs.

"This is mighty pig," announced Asteria with an approving nod. "He was successful pig in life, no doubt."

"Glad you like it," said Hargle. "It's got a fine glaze on it too."

"We will all feast greatly tonight, like queens."

Hargle and Bargle exchanged a wary look.

Asteria shrugged. "Or kings if you like, I suppose."

Hargle and Bargle smiled and nodded. "Good ham-eating weather anyway, I'd say." And then everyone looked out the windows, where the snow fell steadily and the street was packed with it. Gidget the Goblin Girl slept on her display still, snoring peacefully with a twitch here or there.

One by one, more guests arrived. Dave the forlorn

doorman showed up, bringing a cask of good ale. "This isn't the stuff they sell at the Bloody Stump, you can be sure of that," he said, patting the wooden barrel while carrying it on his shoulder.

"I think we can all be thankful for that," said Maribella, and Asteria helped Dave with the cask, easily taking it off his hands.

Several other townspeople arrived, many of them bringing pies and cakes and bread and butter and salt and wines and all manner of delicious things to eat and drink. Soon, the Cozy Quill Bookshop was full of people and conversation and laughter. The sound of a flute rang out, and faces lit up and everyone clapped along at a jaunty little ditty. Then the musician switched to a slower, melancholy tune, and everyone settled in and drank their drinks and warmed their hands by one fire or another, and even may have held a loved one closer.

Captain Hargle and Captain Bargle argued over the serving of dinner. Both wanted to be in charge of doling out the ham, and they worked it out eventually.

"Ham?" said one of them, offering a big plate of it to Maribella.

"Uh," she said, involuntarily wincing. "Not just now, thank you." Then she went to go and eat something that wasn't meat.

Asteria gorged herself, of course, and for the first time she seemed to really be engaging with the townspeople without the need for Maribella to be present as the middle ground. She was glad to see the sight.

Almost like the place is becoming a home for her, she thought.

While Maribella was putting more wood in the fire there was a knock at the door, and she went to answer it. "Coming!" When she opened the door she came face to face with a smiling sloth staring deeply into her eyes.

Catalina the Llama Merchant also stood there, of course.

She held Esteban the sloth.

"Catalina!" said Maribella, lighting up in a smile. "You came. Oh, I'm ever so glad. And all the llamas are here too." Several llamas standing in the street grunted in response.

"Leafhaven is on my route back south," said Catalina with a shrug. "So I figured I'd wait out the rest of winter here. Esteban missed you."

And then Esteban produced a single flower hidden beneath him in his clawed, slothy hand.

"Oh, *well* then," said Maribella, taking the flower. "Thank you very much, Esteban."

"Here, hold him for a bit," said Catalina, and she handed the sloth to Maribella before entering the bookshop.

Maribella and Esteban stared into each others eyes and they had quite the moment.

Eventually, Maribella went and found Asteria, who sat in a chair near the fireplace. She was smoking a pipe, which was something she normally didn't do, but Captain Bargle had talked her into it and so now she looked quite comfy. Maribella stood next to her chair, and with Asteria sitting, their faces were of the same height and they could talk conspiratorially.

"Look at that," said Maribella as Esteban tried to reach out and grab Asteria's spiky hair. "She already found Dave." They watched as Catalina and Dave chatted across the room. Catalina had a smile, and Dave looked red-faced and very caught off guard.

"Hmm," murmured Asteria. "She came back into his life after all. It is like I said. People come. People go. And sometimes those people come again."

Both women's eyebrows rose when Catalina pulled flowers from a satchel and offered them to Dave.

"She gave him flowers!" whispered Maribella, grabbing onto Asteria's shoulder and leaning into her. "Just like how Dave gave her flowers when she left! Look at them!"

"Falling stars," said Asteria in awe. "It is actually happening for Dave. He has wooed llama girl."

Just then there was another knock at the door, this one louder than the knock before. As sad as she was to miss the spectacle happening across the room, Maribella pulled away to answer the door, but not before handing off Esteban to Asteria.

She opened the door. Nobody was there.

"Huh, that's odd," said Maribella.

She shut the door and began to walk away when there came another knock. She whirled around and opened the door to once again find nobody there but the llamas tied up nearby.

"How very strange," said Maribella.

"Oi! Love!" called a tiny woman's voice. "Set your peepers down here."

Maribella looked down to find a worm on the porch looking up at her. This worm resembled Mr Reginald Cumberbutton, complete with thick glasses enlarging big eyes. The main difference was where Mr Cumberbutton was bald, this new worm actually had hair, and it was quite done up in a chic and fashionable bob style.

"Oh!" cried Maribella. "But it's another bookworm!"

"Yeah, that's right," nodded the lady bookworm.

"But how is it you knocked on the door like that? And how and why are you even here?"

The worm looked up at Maribella with big eyes and an open mouth.

Maribella looked down at the worm.

Several seconds passed.

"You wot?"

"Apologies," said Maribella. "It's just, well, I've never had a bookworm come and knock on my door before."

The worm looked around as if she had gotten the wrong place. "This is the Cozy Quill Bookshop, innit?"

"Why yes, it is."

"You havin' a go at me? You askin' why a bloody bookworm shows up to a bloody bookshop? You havin' a laugh?"

"Why, no miss bookworm!" And she winced as soon as the words left her mouth.

"You wot? My name isn't miss bookworm, miss human. It's Ms Henrietta Appletop, and I'm a big deal in the bookworm community, why I am."

"I am dearly sorry, Ms Appletop."

"Why my standin' in the cold still, then?"

"Apologies. Here you are." Maribella bent down and placed her hand flat on the ground and waited for the bookworm to slowly crawl onto her palm.

"More like it," said Ms Appletop as she crawled. "Some right proper transportation, this is."

Maribella carefully brought her inside and carried her through the bookshop, and every guest she passed looked on with great interest.

"Evenin'" nodded Ms Appletop to several townspeople. "Lovely Winter Solstice party you're havin'. Smells right fine and dandy it does. There we are now, on the front desk is fine."

Maribella let off the bookworm at the desk where she had a good view of the party.

"There we are," said Ms Appletop.

"Can I get you anything to eat? A nice cider or plate of ham?"

"You wot?"

"Are you hungry?"

"Aye, I'm a mite peckish. I could go for some good aged dust, if you have it."

"We do."

"Fetch me your dustiest book then, if it pleases."

Minutes later, Maribella and Asteria and others gathered around to watch the new bookworm lapping at dust on the cover of a book.

"Right tasty book, this is," she said. "Turns out the rumors of this bookshop proved true."

"Oh?" said Maribella. "You've heard of the shop?"

"Why I'm here, it is. Any good bookshop worth its dust is

going to get talked about in any respectable bookworm society."

"I see."

"Good thing I got here early as I did. Grueling journey it was, but made it I did."

"Well I'm happy to have you as a guest. You can stay as long as you like. And if I can, I'd also like to say that you're not the first bookworm we've had the pleasure of welcoming here. There's another bookworm upstairs. One Mr Reginald Cumberbutton."

Ms Appletop looked up at Maribella with a gaping mouth. "You wot?"

"I said there's another bookworm in the building right this very moment."

Ms Appletop's spectacled eyes moved from Maribella to Asteria. "A gentleman bookworm is here?"

"He is."

"Is he handsome?"

Maribella exchanged a look with Asteria.

"Yes," said Asteria.

And here Ms Appletop looked a bit nervous suddenly, as if caught off guard. She fidgeted and stared about aimlessly. Her myriads of little legs wiggled back and forth. "How do I look?" she asked.

"Very presentable," said Maribella.

"Well then. There's nothin' else to it, I suppose. Go and fetch him and let's be done with it."

Maribella raced upstairs, fascinated by the turn of events and eager to see how they would play out. She entered Mr Cumberbutton's room and announced herself and then explained the entire situation.

"You wot?" said Mr Cumberbutton.

Maribella explained it all again.

"Oh, well then, all right," said the bookworm, fidgeting and looking down at himself. "How do I look?"

"Very presentable," said Maribella.

"Right then. Oh, but this is all so sudden. But very well.

Take me down to see her."

Maribella transported Mr Cumberbutton to the first floor in the same manner she did Ms Appletop. He looked about the place, wide-eyed and open-mouthed.

She placed him a few feet away from Ms Appletop on the desk and introduced them. "Ms Henrietta Appletop, this is Mr Reginald Cumberbutton."

Both worms stared at each other with their mouths gaping open.

Neither said a word.

And then, out of nowhere, they both began to race toward each other.

Race in a very liberal sense. They slowly crawled toward each other. Inch by slow inch. They said nothing, but their faces were glued in each other's direction, and tiny panting came out of their O-shaped mouths.

"What are they doing?" whispered Captain Hargle.

"Running toward each other," said Dave.

"To what end?" asked Captain Bargle.

"They look so very focused," said Catalina.

The bookworms slowly drew closer, and Maribella leaned in to see better.

"What do you think will happen?" asked Clarence.

"They will fight," said Asteria. "This is display of force over territory. Such things happen among moose. This is so."

Closer and closer they got.

Ever closer.

And then.

They kissed.

Maribella lit up in a smile. "Look at that! Oh, but how romantic, isn't it? They're hitting it off so very well."

Townspeople scrunched up their faces and watched as the two bookworms continued to kiss.

"They progressed rather fast, wouldn't you say?" said Hargle.

"Well, perhaps bookworms have short lives so they need

to work quickly," said Maribella. "Whatever the case, I think it's beautiful. Magical, even. How likely was it that poor Mr Cumberbutton, locked away up in his room, hidden away from the world all day, would find true love like this? I think it's a wonderful lesson to learn from these two. Love is always possible, even when you think it's not."

Maribella couldn't help but scan her eyes across the small crowd, lingering on Dave and Catalina who stood very close together. And of course, her gaze also fell on Asteria. When Asteria looked at her, she looked away.

For several seconds, the entire party stood silently inside the Cozy Quill Bookshop and watched the bookworms.

They were still kissing.

Maribella cleared her throat, and then coughed into her hand. It was a fake cough.

The kissing progressed to a level of crudeness I will not convey here. Suffice to say, it got pretty disturbing.

"Um," said Maribella. "Okay then, let's give them some privacy, I suppose. That's enough, everyone. Let's get back to the party."

"They're still going at it," said Dave.

Maribella had to get a platter lid to cover the worms and get everyone's attention off them, and finally the celebration was allowed to go back to its normal cheeriness.

Someone had gotten a lute and taken over for the flute, and the lutist now played slow and quiet songs. Conversation calmed to a low din, and people shared drinks around fireplaces and braziers. It almost felt like a quaint and well-mannered tavern in the bookshop.

As Maribella made the rounds, she heard people murmuring nearby the main first floor fireplace.

"Rumor is," said one, "the Ha-Mazan Tribes are retreating now. Fraey Tarta went and actually fought them off!"

"Rumor is," said another, "the King of Fraey Tarta is to

thank for that. He mustered the entire kingdom to defend the border."

"Aye, but rumor is," said yet another, "the Queen of Fraey Tarta is sicker than ever, still confined to her bed. They say she may very well go and die."

There were many things Maribella felt just then. Things both happy and sad.

When she looked at Asteria, sitting in a chair nearby the rumormongers, her spirits darkened. Asteria looked suddenly solemn after hearing the news. Maribella went to her.

"How are you enjoying the celebration?" she asked.

Asteria might as well have been in another world completely. When she spoke, she spoke softly and to herself more than anyone else.

"The Tribes are falling back to their lands," she said.

Maribella didn't know what to say. It was good news, but still, a seed of anxiety grew in her heart.

Asteria looked off into the distance. "I can no longer defy fate. I must accept it."

And all at once, Maribella was whisked away once again to the third floor tower the day they had discovered it, and the things Asteria had said. How fate was the most important thing to a Ha-Mazan person. How it was her fate to spend her life defending her Queen. How she had denied that fate when coming to Leafhaven, and how defying her fate lay heavily on her soul.

Maribella was unable so speak.

"My Queen may still take me back," whispered Asteria, her eyes focused hundreds of miles away. "She may take me back. I may live out my fate after all. I must leave soon."

"Asteria," said Maribella, stepping closer.

Asteria looked at her with the reaction of someone being pulled away from something very important.

"Uh," said Maribella. "I was going to give you this later, but I think now would be better." She didn't know what she was doing. It just felt right to do it now, though. "Hold on a moment."

She dashed to her bedroom and came back down with a wrapped present.

"What is this?" asked Asteria.

"It's a present."

"What for?"

"Well, sometimes people like to give presents to others on the Winter Solstice. It's not required or anything, but sometimes people do it."

"Why did you not tell me? I have no present to give back."

"Oh, it's quite all right." Maribella awkwardly laughed and rubbed at the back of her head. She felt uncharacteristically frazzled for some reason. "You don't have to get me anything. I just wanted to give you this is all."

Asteria inspected the wrapped object. It had a bow on it, and it was shaped like a book. She arched her brow and gave Maribella a look. "I wonder what it could be."

Maribella couldn't decide if Asteria was being sarcastic or not, since she had never once ever heard a single sarcastic thing come out of the woman's mouth. But there's a first for everything.

Asteria tore the paper off. "A book."

"But not just any book. Here, read the title."

"*Reading Improvement*," said Asteria. "What is this?"

"It's an educational book for someone who knows the basics of reading but could improve their reading skills, such as yourself. You were always saying how you didn't like that you were a slow reader. So now this might help you. It was made for someone just like you."

Asteria flipped the book over and looked at it from different angles.

Maribella felt her face go red. She gave a nervous laugh and looked at her feet. "I know. It's stupid. You don't have to ever read it if you don't want, but it's something you can keep around. It's a dumb present, I know."

Asteria said nothing. Heavy silence sat between them.

At length, Maribella looked up.

Asteria had tears in her eyes.

Maribella's heart skipped a beat. She had never seen Asteria cry before. "What's wrong? Is something the matter? You're crying."

"Ha-Mazan warriors do not cry," said Asteria, holding the book closer. "We shed tears. And you are wrong. It is not dumb present." She looked up from the book. "It is the best thing anyone has given me."

She reached out and wrapped her arms around Maribella, pulling her in.

They embraced for a long while. Maribella felt so small in Asteria's arms. She was strong and warm.

When they parted, their faces were very close to each other.

"I..." said Maribella, her heart racing.

Asteria said nothing. She cast her tortured gaze into Maribella's own.

"I...I need to see to the guests," said Maribella, and hurried away.

Maribella sat with Clarence near the front of the shop, watching snow gently fall on the street.

"It's certainly a snowy Winter Solstice this year," said Clarence.

"Yes," said Maribella.

"I always did like to sit and watch the snow." Party guests chatted quietly behind them throughout the bookshop, but the street was empty and still. Beside them lay Gidget, still fast asleep on her display table. "Sometimes life seems so fast, but you can always count on snow to slow it down. I've lived here such a long time, and I've seen many a snowy night like this. You'd think it'd get old, but it's not. Even when the people you watch the snow with change, the view stays the same."

"Yes." Maribella wasn't so much watching the snow as she was staring through it.

They stayed silent for a long while. As far as Maribella was concerned, she could have stayed silent for an eternity.

"Are you happy?" asked Clarence.

Maribella gave him a questioning stare.

"With your shop," continued Clarence. "With the purchase. You bought the place. Came to town. Opened it back up. It's a success now. Are you happy with it?"

Maribella thought for a moment, and then answered with a soft voice. "Yes."

"That's good. That's good."

They went back to watching the snow fall.

"I was wondering," said Clarence.

"Yes?"

"In your bedroom, would there happen to be a small painting of a lovely young woman hanging on the wall?"

Clarence turned to Maribella, a curious look on his face.

"Why yes, there is," said Maribella.

He smiled. "That's good to hear. Tell me, do you think it would be possible for you to humor an old fool and bring it down so I can look at it?"

Maribella thought it an extremely strange request, and as she walked up the stairs to her bedroom it only grew more and more strange in her head. *Why ever would Clarence be interested in a painting of a random woman in my bedroom?*

She took the painting off its hook and brought it down to the first floor. It looked much the same as it did the first time she found it. The face of a pretty young woman with curly hair smiled at the painter.

"Here you are," said Maribella, handing it to Clarence and sitting back down.

He held it and stared at it.

"How did you know it was in my bedroom?" Maribella gave a little laugh. "You haven't been sneaking about the place, have you?"

"Oh, no, nothing like that." He ran his hand down the frame of the picture. "It's where she said she put it, is all."

"Where who said?"

"The woman in the painting, of course."

Maribella looked at the painting. "The previous owner."

"That's right. The previous owner. From many years ago, before she grew old and died."

Maribella felt a heaviness fall over them both. She sank further into her chair, staring at the woman's eyes with newfound appreciation. "You knew her well."

"I did."

"It's a lovely painting."

"I know. I'm the one who painted it."

Maribella looked to Clarence, open-mouthed. "You..."

When Clarence finally pried his gaze from the woman in the painting and looked back to Maribella, his eyes were full of tears. "I had my flower shop for as long as she had this bookshop," he said, his voice shaking just a bit. "A few buildings away, we were. I brought her flowers, and she loaned me books."

Maribella bit her bottom lip, unable to say anything.

"'Tomorrow', I would say," continued Clarence. "'Tomorrow, I will do it. There is still time tomorrow. Not today. Tomorrow.' And then one day, there was no tomorrow for her. It's been twenty years now since that tomorrow went away." He turned back to the painting of the Cozy Quill's former owner. "I waited too long, Maribella. I waited too long, and now I only have this painting. Life moves fast. Faster than you could ever imagine. The days go by, the months go by, the years go by. So very fast they go by. Don't wait for tomorrow, Maribella. Don't find yourself with only a memory to hold onto."

Maribella swallowed, holding back her own tears.

The front door softly knocked.

"A guest," she said, forcing herself to get up. "So late in the evening. I must answer the door, Clarence."

Her mind was still reeling when she opened the door to find Lady Malicent standing behind it.

A blast of wintry snow blew into the shop, sending book pages fluttering and guests squinting. Far away beyond the borders of town flashed lightning in dark clouds, illuminating the silhouette of Lady Malicent and her tall, pointy hennin. She glared down at Maribella, and Maribella gaped up at her.

"Lady Malicent," she said. "To what do I owe—"

"Don't say a word," said Lady Malicent. "Any word uttered from your mouth is entirely unneeded."

Maribella obliged and waited silently for Malicent to make a point.

But she didn't make a point.

She stepped aside to reveal a large group of men behind her.

More thunder and lightning cracked and flashed in the distance, and the men barreled their way inside the bookshop. Maribella stood to the side, watching as half a dozen of them filed in. These weren't Lady Malicent's goons. They didn't wear simple cloaks and they weren't armed with clubs. They donned expensive armor and wore steel at their hips.

"Whatever is the meaning of this?" asked Maribella as she moved to the front desk to address the new group.

Asteria drew near her side. "Shall I go and get table for sale?" she whispered.

"No, you will not," said Maribella. "And you men. Answer me at once. What are you—"

Her voice caught in her throat when a man with the aura of *power* strode into the bookshop. Lady Malicent waited behind him, following in his wake. Behind *her* was Miles, her personal goon, wearing the same self-satisfied expression as his mistress.

The stranger was in his thirties, tall and lean with broad shoulders, a square jaw, and a gaze that would make an eagle tremble in his feathers. He wore a cape that fluttered behind him, and his finely shined boots thumped heavily on the floorboards. Everything about his outfit was immaculate and expensive, and he had the authoritative demeanor to match.

"It's common for commoners to bow, or at least curtsy when they're in the presence of nobility," he said.

Maribella looked around and only now noticed that all the guests had taken to a knee, their heads down.

Maribella did a quick curtsy. "I take it you're Baron Blauca," she said.

"I am."

"Well it's about time you showed up. I've been trying to get a hold of you for weeks and weeks. I tried visiting your manor. I've sent a dozen letters. I'm turned away and ignored at every attempt."

"Stop," said Blauca, raising a hand.

Behind him Lady Malicent grinned a wide, wicked smile, her mouth stretching far across her face. "Oh, little bookshop girl. How delicious it is to see you in such a precarious position. You don't even know how much trouble you're in, do you?"

"Trouble?" asked Maribella.

"Yes, *trouble*," said Baron Blauca, and he took one imposing step forward. Maribella shrank back. "It turns out we have a *problem*. A very *large* problem. One that requires my own personal intervention. Something I must put to rights at *once*, right now, tonight, at this very moment.

"A...problem?"

She was pushed back to her desk and Blauca drew closer and closer, eventually stooping over her. "Yes, a problem. One that *you will address right now.*"

Maribella swallowed quite audibly.

And then Blauca said, "The Baroness Blauca is expecting a Winter Solstice gift tonight, and she is *impossible* to shop for." He smiled and exhaled and shook his head and rubbed at the back of that same head and then turned about looking at the place. "Which is where you and your wonderful bookshop come in."

"My what?" asked Maribella.

"Her what?" asked a stricken Malicent.

"Her what?" asked Miles the goon.

"Her what?" asked everyone else.

"Her bookshop," said Asteria.

Blauca addressed the crowd of onlookers. "Did I muffle my words? I said I need a gift, for my wife, this very moment, tonight. And this bookshop is the perfect place to shop for her."

Maribella blinked her eyes several times, then shook her head and gathered herself. "Uh, of course, Baron Blauca. What is it the Baroness is interested in?"

"Ah. Yes. Her interests. You see, she's extremely difficult to please, my beloved. If I get her a gift that displeases her I'll be hearing about it for weeks. She might even get bitey. But what do you get a woman who can buy anything she wants? That's where *rarity* comes in."

"Rarity?"

"Yes. You see, my wife claims to be a big reader of books. She brags to all of her friends about this. But in reality she doesn't like reading at all. She simply likes to collect the most expensive, rarest, oldest editions of books there are. Now, this bookshop is very old, and I know the inventory is still in here from the previous owner from twenty years ago. So there has to be something here that would impress her and her friends. Remember now, I'm looking for a book, and it doesn't matter how well-written or accurate or worthwhile the actual words in this book are. All that matters is that it's very old and very expensive. Price is no concern to me. Do you have anything like this?"

Well, dear reader?

Does she?

Maribella and Asteria pointed at each other at the very same time with wide eyes, and in unison they said, "Isambard Ruskin's *The Excursion of the One Who Longs to Penetrate the Curtains of the Strange*!"

Maribella grabbed the Baron by the sleeve, forgetting all decorum, and brought him to the altar with the glass box that contained the ancient tome inside.

"My word," he said. "I've heard of this. Copies this old are extremely rare."

"Yes, indeed," said Maribella, beaming with pride. "It's a plodding book, and the Baroness will never have to actually read it. But just look at it. Her friends will be oh so very jealous."

"It is like rotting beaver log," added Asteria helpfully. "It is awful book and very expensive."

"There, there, Asteria. That'll do. So then, Baron. Will this be adequate?"

The Baron rose his brows. "I should think so! What a wonderful find, this is. Why, this is better than I could have hoped to imagine. I love this bookshop!"

And the crowd of onlookers cheered. Mugs of ale were clashed together and several fully grown men embraced one another with joy.

The roar of an angry cougar put an end to the celebration.

Lady Malicent stepped forward, fuming, her jaw clenched and her nostrils flared. "*Blauca*. What is the meaning of this?"

"Excuse me?" said the Baron in a tone that sounded like he had completely forgotten about Malicent.

"I brought you here tonight to kick this woman off my property, not give her business and good reviews."

"Oh, well I'm sorry for the confusion. I came here for a gift for my demanding wife. Yes, this find will stop her from draining my blood anytime soon, the vampiress."

"But look!" Lady Malicent slapped down documentation showing she owned the land the Cozy Quill was built on. "This land is mine. I fully intend on tearing down this eyesore and building my tenements in its place."

Maribella stepped forward, quick to draw out her own documentation, signed by Blauca himself, showing the sale of the Cozy Quill to Maribella Waters. "Yes, about that. I have documentation of ownership as well."

"Ah. Yes," said Blauca. "This messy business. I had meant to get around to this. You see, this was all a great misunderstanding. Apparently there were many business deals taking place about twenty years ago when the previous owner of the shop died. Not everything was properly filed, and there were some mix-ups. It was the bookkeepers' fault, really." (Baron Blauca was correct in blaming the bookkeepers, they had made many errors.) "So, somehow House Malicent came into ownership of the land, and ownership of the shop itself was in the name of the Barony for twenty years, then sold to Ms Waters here, for far less than it was worth, might I add. Now, we must resolve the issue. Unless the two of you want to hash out a renting agreement...?"

He paused, waiting for one of the women to bite, but neither did.

"...then I'll have to step in and make an executive decision. And let it be said here and now my decision is this: the Cozy Quill is to be regarded as a historical treasure to be preserved to time indefinite, and full ownership of the land it sits on is to be transferred to Ms Maribella Waters."

The crowd cheered for a good long while.

Lady Malicent stepped forward, seething and raging, her clawed hand crushing the deed to the land. "This is outrageous."

Maribella smiled up at Baron Blauca. "And here I thought you were going to do whatever Lady Malicent told you to do."

"Who, me?" said Blauca. "Of course not. What gave you that idea?"

"The rumors are you're under her thumb."

"Pshaw, the only woman's thumb I'm under is my wife's, the blood-sucker. Lady Malicent is merely an annoying aristocrat who thinks her word is more powerful than it is."

"My family paid for this land years ago," said Malicent, a quiver in her voice. "This is entirely unfair."

"I agree," said Blauca. "A grave misdeed has been done to you, Lady Malicent. I am sorry it happened, and I mean to rectify it right here and now. You will be given a tract of land double the size of the land this bookshop sits on. The land will be located just at the edge of town where new development is going up, and you will be given express permission to build whatever your heart's desire wants."

"But," said Malicent, looking as if she didn't know what to say now. "But the shop...I was going to tear it down."

Blauca arched an eyebrow. "And? Now you don't have to. Now you have twice the land and permission to build. You've made out very well in all of this, Jeanie. Don't go and throw a fit just because it didn't play out exactly like you wanted it to."

Lady Malicent lowered her head and stood silent and still.

Chatter in the bookshop started up again, and things began to relax. Maribella and Blauca stood and talked near his new purchase.

"Yes, those damned bookkeepers," Blauca was saying. "They also made the mistake of severely underselling this bookshop. That's how you got it so cheap. They thought they were selling you an empty barn."

"I'll forever bless bookkeepers, then," said Maribella.

"But it's quite all right in the end. I don't mind. This bookshop needs a manager I can trust, someone to curate it. I think you've proven your worth. True, I could have gotten a much greater sum of money for the place, but I think I can sleep fine at night knowing you're at the helm here."

"I feel just a bit silly selling you your own expensive book right back."

"Think nothing of it. I like to delegate. I'm a busy man. Consider that purchase a reward for watching over this shop, and helping me find the perfect gift within. It all worked out in the end, didn't it?"

"Indeed it did. But I don't understand. I tried so hard to get a hold of you. I visited your manor. I sent letters. Why didn't you reach back out when you could have solved this all so easily?"

"Ah, well there's an easy explanation for that. I was traveling, you see. Our very own King sent me on a diplomatic quest to our neighbors on the border to see the King of Fraey Tarta."

"Oh."

"He just achieved victory over the Ha-Mazan invaders, so it was a celebration all around." He nodded to Asteria. "No offense."

"None taken," said Asteria.

"But yes, that's where I've been. Relations improved, so that's good. I believe we may have started the beginnings of an alliance against future threats. Too bad about his young wife, though. Just married, they were, and then she goes and gets deathly ill. I wasn't even able to meet her, it's so bad. I think he'll be looking for a new wife soon."

Maribella looked down and bit her lip, and when she looked back up her eyes found Lady Malicent. She still stood in the same spot as before, and hadn't moved an inch. Maribella had expected her to have stormed off in a fit of rage by now, with Miles her goon close behind.

But she just stood there.

And she wasn't looking down.

She was looking toward a bookshelf.

Maribella stepped forward tentatively. "Is there anything —"

Malicent ignored her and took a single step toward the shelf. "You have..." She trailed off.

Maribella tried to spot what she was fixated on, but there were so many books. "Yes?"

"You have them..."

She moved to the bookshelf.

She placed her hands on a series of books that all had a similar make.

"You have them..."

Maribella gently drew near. There was a temporary feeling of standing next to an unchained hungry lion, but it passed. Lady Malicent was just a woman, after all.

"You have them..."

Silently, Maribella looked at Malicent's hand where it lay on the *Lady Jeanie Mysteries* collection.

"You have every last one..."

Maribella then looked up to Malicent's face.

A single tear streaked down her cheek.

"...even the ones I never got to read."

"I..." whispered Maribella, not sure what to say.

And then came the tapping of canes on the wooden floor.

"I remember now," said Clarence, huffing as he drew close. "I remember now. I remember it like it was yesterday. The manservant. I remember what he bought now, whenever he came to visit the bookshop. He was always on the lookout for the latest Lady Jeanie book. And I remember which House he belonged to as well."

Lady Malicent closed her eyes.

"House Malicent," said Clarence. "It was a manservant of House Malicent who came by so often, so long ago. Oh, twenty years and more, now. Why, Lady Malicent, you would have been a good ten years old at that time, wouldn't you? Just a little girl."

"Yes," she whispered.

"It was you, wasn't it? It was you that sent out the manservant to the bookshop. It was you that was always on the lookout for the latest Lady Jeanie book. You were a young noblewoman just like her. Why, you even have her same first name."

The entire bookshop grew deathly silent, and all eyes were focused on the noblewoman.

"Yes," said Malicent at last. "Funny that, isn't it? She was what I always wanted to be. She lived the life I wished I could have lived. She broke free from her restrictive parents. She had adventures. She was so well-loved. I adored these books. I read them all, over and over, and always bought the newest one. And then the bookshop owner went and died. And then my manservant said there was nobody to buy from anymore. And then I pleaded with my father to buy the shop. And then he bought the land, but refused to—in his own words—'waste a single copper bit on something as foolish as a bookshop'."

She ran her hands along the collection of books.

"And so I couldn't read anymore. I was physically trapped before, and now I was finally completely trapped. Oh, how I hated her so. How I hated the woman who died and imprisoned me. Why couldn't she stay alive? Why couldn't she have kept the shop open? And then, all these years later, what is it I hear? Twenty years later, what becomes all the rage? The talk of the town? The Cozy Quill. Everyone coming here and buying books and enjoying it all so very much. As if it was the most normal and mundane thing in the world. As if it wasn't something special to be cherished. They didn't know what it was to lose it all. And so I was going to show them."

She let her head drop, and she clenched her fist. At length, she turned to Maribella with tears in her eyes.

"I'll buy the entire collection," she said. "Double the price is only fitting. And I am so very, very sorry, Maribella."

"You see?" said Asteria to Miles the hired goon. "Some books have pictures in them like this one."

"Oooh," said Miles. The two of them shared a table, admiring lush drawings of landscapes and castles and knights. "And here I thought they were full of only words."

"Me as well. There are many such pictures in some books."

"Fascinatin', 'tis."

The mood was now cheerier than ever. It was late, and the guests should have gone home long ago, but they hadn't and Maribella didn't mind at all.

Have you ever had a holiday celebration where someone drank entirely too much alcohol and did something they would normally never do? Several guests were currently doing that. One elderly woman who baked bread down the road was regaling some tavern goers with jokes that were quite raunchy and entirely unfit for these wholesome pages.

"But what about the one where Lady Jeanie finds out the man was never murdered at all, but just died slipping during a fit of rage by himself, and everyone thought he was murdered because he fell and broke his neck?" asked Maribella, sipping at her tea.

"*Lady Jeanie and the Snapped Secretary*," said Lady

Malicent, pouring herself some more tea. "I always preferred it when there was a murderer to pin it on. What's the fun when there's no villain?"

"But it was so unexpected!"

Many women had surrounded Baron Blauca. Despite his frequent references to his wife (who Maribella was seriously starting to think might have been a real vampiress), he seemed to relish the attention.

"Of course I've seen my fair share of battle," he said, leaning on a table's edge, swirling a goblet of wine. "Oh, back in my youth I slayed a whole pile of trolls. Vile creatures, they are. Always demanding transportation taxes and whatnot. I mean *we* built the bloody bridges. If anybody should be taxing them it's us!"

"What if you were to hire the trolls as your tax collectors so they report to you?" asked one industrious woman.

"My word, what an idea. I like you."

The party continued late into the night, and then one by one, each guest grew silent.

No, not because they were starting to fall asleep. Quite the opposite. They were now more awake than they had ever been all night.

For we have now come to the climax of the Winter Solstice, the zenith of the night which is the zenith of the year.

The last man went quiet, and now everyone watched the little goblin girl walk her way toward a table with an empty chair. She carried a mug of steaming tea in one hand, and a town flier with all the news in the other.

Gidget the Goblin Girl was awake and walking about.

Captain Hargle rubbed his eyes and opened them wide, blinking in disbelief.

This entire time, during her entire stay at the Cozy Quill, Gidget had never once been witnessed getting up from her display table.

Everyone watched in perfectly silent awe.

She pulled out the chair and hopped up on it, ignoring the

crowd as if they weren't even there. She blew at her tea, then sipped at it, slurping quite loudly, and then let out a mighty, "*Ah*."

Her hand flicked the news flier and straightened it out, and she started reading, intermittently sipping at her tea and going, "*Ah*," after every sip.

"Some flooding down in Rivermont this season, looks like," she said after reading the headline.

Everyone looked at each other, then back to the goblin girl.

"Corn prices are up. Huh." She sipped at her tea again.

This went on for a very long time. She drank her tea and randomly spouted news headlines. After several minutes, she set down an empty mug and grunted and stood up. She tucked the news flier under an arm and began to walk for the rear door.

"*Welp*," she said, finally acknowledging the gawkers. "I'll be in the latrine for a while. Nobody bother me."

The whole room let out an exhale when Gidget left, and chatter once again commenced.

Maribella smiled, and she suddenly felt so very tired. It was quite past her usual bedtime, after all.

"You know what?" she said to whoever was around. "I do believe this has been the best Winter Solstice I've ever had. I'm going to bed."

Chapter 22

Maribella Gets an Unwanted Visit

It had been several days since the Winter Solstice, and already the town was installing decorations for New Year's Night. It wouldn't be long now until the whole kingdom would bring in the new year with much music, laughter, drink and general celebration.

What's that? Leafhaven certainly does have a lot of festivals and celebrations, you say? Well we should all be thankful for that! Imagine a place where life simply rolls along at the same drab rhythm it always does, with no special days to break things up and no events to look forward to. If you happen to live in a place or with people who don't celebrate things in general, then I advise you to try to leave that place and find new and better people the first chance you get.

And so Maribella watched the town nail up colorful strings of lantern decorations from one side of the street to the other as she shoveled snow from the front porch to the Cozy Quill. It had been a windy snowfall the previous night, so the awning didn't do much to protect the porch. Normally this sort of labor was reserved for Asteria, who could accomplish it in a fraction of the time it took Maribella, but Maribella felt like getting up and doing something and so there she was, puffing out clouds of air while tossing snow off the porch.

Many people passed by in the street. She watched them casually as anyone would do. Not a single one stood out in any specific way or manner.

Until the man with the cloak and sword showed up.

His shoulders were bulky underneath the cloak, betraying the armor he wore. At his hip was a fine sword, finer even than any weapon the Baron's guards wore. He walked with the stature of a proud knight, but he wore no House coat of arms that would tell his allegiance.

Maribella quickly looked away as he strolled down the street. In her side vision she saw him stop and stare at her.

He stepped up onto the porch and Maribella made an effort to turn away from him, focusing on shoveling snow.

"My lady," he said. "Is that you?"

She ignored him.

"My lady," he said, and touched the side of her arm.

She whipped about and glanced at him. "You've mistaken me for someone else. I've never met you in my life."

A confused smile came over the man's face, and he shook his head. "My lady, please cease with these games. I've finally found you. We've been searching for months. You must come with me right away."

Maribella tossed the next shovel of snow in his direction.

He didn't bother dodging out of the way and the snow hit him in the legs. "My lady, please come with me now. I must bring you back."

"You have me confused with someone else," said Maribella. "It happens often with me."

"I most certainly do not have you confused with someone else."

"The bookshop is closing early today right now, you must leave." She turned away from him and began to walk inside, even though there was still plenty of snow on the porch.

She felt a firm grip squeeze her upper arm, stopping her.

She looked up and came face to face with a determined young man. "My lady," he said softly.

Just then the door to the bookshop swung open and Asteria emerged holding a small table. "I have fine table for sale," she said. "Please good sir, do take a look and perhaps purchase this fine table for sale."

The man let go of Maribella and glared at Asteria. "So then. You've gone and hired some Ha-Mazan muscle. The gall of it." He backed away, his face now displaying much anger, snapping between the two women. "If that's how you wish to play it, so be it. Stay here if you like. I will let him know, though. *He* will decide what to do."

The man walked away, disappearing down the street.

"Who is this man?" asked Asteria, still holding the table.

Maribella watched his back until he was out of her vision. "I don't know. I've never met him in my life." She turned and went inside. "Just a confused man is all."

Chapter 23

Leafhaven Celebrates New Year's Night

It was almost midnight, a crackling of energy was in the air, and Asteria was nowhere to be found.

Maribella looked all over the bookshop, but there was no seven-foot barbarian anywhere. She even searched the bookworms' room, but only found the two bookworms sharing a book.

"Ain't no Asteria in here, love, just us kids," said Mr Cumberbutton, and then went back to sucking on Ms Appletop's face.

And so Maribella took to the streets, walking fast enough to make her huff and puff misty air. There was no more falling snow, but plenty of it fresh on the ground, and it crunched under her boots.

"The dawn of a new year," Asteria had ominously whispered to herself just the day before while looking off into the distance. "The time for great changes."

Maribella hadn't liked that kind of talk at *all*, but she didn't speak up. She had ignored the issue, relying on the fact that Asteria would always be there, big and dependable, always standing by her side whenever a problem arose.

Except now she wasn't.

The town was pulsing with an air of expectant energy. It was that special time of night just before towns and cities all over the land would send off their fireworks into the black sky to celebrate another birthday of all existence. Smiling people roamed the streets in pairs and groups, toasting wine glasses or blowing noise makers or singing joyful songs. Flutes and lutes and drums echoed in the distance, one band competing against another depending on which street you stood on.

Maribella headed for Peabush Square in the center of town, where most of the celebration would be taking place. She thought maybe Asteria just got a head start on the festivities. On her way there she passed by Clarence's flower shop where he sat out on the porch.

"Going to the Square?" asked the old man from his rocking chair. "It's too big and busy for me, these days. I can enjoy the fireworks just fine from my porch."

"I'm looking for Asteria, actually. Have you seen her?"

"I haven't. But keep looking, I'm sure you'll find her in the crowd. Not many seven-feet tall women around, after all."

Maribella took that to heart, searching for a head towering over everyone else. She didn't find it. But she did come across a procession of llama's tied up just before an entrance to the Square. Catalina sat on a box doing business with the crowd, and Dave stood next to her and assisted.

"Hey Maribella!" he shouted with a big smile. "Isn't it an amazing night? I usually spend it manning the door to the Bloody Stump on New Year's Night, and boy is that depressing. But not this year. This year I'm helping Catalina out."

Esteban the sloth hung around his neck at his shoulders, and he gave Maribella a smug smile, as if she should be jealous that he was hanging on Dave and she wasn't.

"That's good to hear and all," said Maribella. She couldn't force a smile. "Have you seen Asteria? I haven't found her all evening. We were supposed to celebrate the new year together."

"Haven't seen her," said Catalina, counting out coins from a customer and dropping them in a small chest. "She's probably getting something to eat. Lots to eat in the Square."

"Oh, yes. Okay, thank you."

Dave grabbed her before she could leave. "Hey, Maribella,"

he said, voice raised over the noisy din of the crowd. "Did you hear the news?"

"What news?"

"I quit my job at the Bloody Stump. I'm going to be setting off with Catalina when she heads out pretty soon. She said she's been looking for someone else to take on, being just her and the animals and all. I'm doing it, Maribella. I'm actually doing it. I'm going to go and see the world, and with Catalina of all people. This might be the happiest I've ever felt. It's going to be one big adventure."

Catalina shrugged and smiled. "I'll see how the greenhorn gets on, maybe I'll keep him."

Maribella was happy for them both, she truly was, but she couldn't feel the happiness in her heart. In fact, there was a tiny bit of strange pain there.

He is leaving town, she thought as she walked away and into the Square. *A little piece of this place is going away, maybe never to come back. A permanent change.*

Peabush Square was absolutely stuffed with people. It seemed the whole town had decided to pack into the place. Aromas of mouth-watering food filled the air, and much drink was had. Noise-makers and music clashed and fought over ear canals, and people jostled each other as a general sort of organized chaos flowed through the area.

Maribella scanned the top of the crowd for a Ha-Mazan warrior, but saw none.

"Ah, there she is!" said Captain Hargle, eating a large turkey leg.

"The town's favorite bookshop owner!" said Captain Bargle, eating an equally large turkey leg.

"Hello Hargle, Bargle." She nodded curtly to both.

"Enjoying the festivities?" asked one of them.

"Indeed I am. But tell me, have either of you seen Asteria around? I seem to have lost her."

"Not at all," said Hargle. "Perhaps ask the Baron? He's up on stage calling the time this year. But you better hurry! It's getting late, and you wouldn't want to miss the fireworks with Asteria, would you?"

Maribella felt like time was running out as she shoved her way through the crowd, fighting to get to the front. She held back curses and gave apologies, and received a few curses herself. By the end of it all she had found her way to the raised wooden platform at one side of the Square. Several important people were on it, chief among them was Baron Blauca talking with some other nobles.

Lady Malicent stood before the crowd on one edge of the platform. She looked quite drunk. Miles her goon held open a bag full of party favors, and Malicent reached in and tossed handfuls to the crowd. She held a mug of beer in her free hand, and she would laugh and drink between throws.

"I do believe they love me!" she called to Maribella as she passed behind. "Have a throw, Maribella. It does wonders for the spirits."

Maribella half-heartedly tossed some cheaply made nicknacks into the crowd, who cheered full-heartedly. She even heard the Cozy Quill's name called out.

"Have you seen Asteria tonight?" she asked Malicent.

"I haven't seen a single Ha-Mazan warrior, my love," said Malicent, already turning her attention back to the crowd.

Finally, Maribella made her way to Baron Blauca.

"There you are," said Blauca, grabbing Maribella by the shoulders and planting her still. "I was hoping you'd show up. You're a notable town figure, Maribella. It's only fitting you stand here with me when I announce the new year. You should be here in the center of all things when the fireworks go off. Now where's that giant friend of yours?"

"That's just what I was going to ask you. Have you seen her?"

"Not a hair of her. Perhaps she doesn't like big, noisy crowds? I heard those Ha-Mazan types can be like that."

Maribella realized that actually made a lot of sense.

The Baron's wife—Baroness Blauca—emerged from

behind the Baron, and Maribella flinched. The noblewoman was tall with black hair and milk-white skin. Her lips were red, her eyes an almost glowing blue, and when she smiled she revealed pronounced canines.

Maribella's eyes went wide.

His wife actually is a vampiress! He wasn't joking around!

"Oh, there's the little bookshop owner, so flushed and pumping with life," said the Baroness. "I've heard much about you. Thank you dearly for providing my Winter Solstice gift, it's given me ever so much to gloat with. Come, Ms Waters, you must visit the manse sometime soon for a..."—she smiled and ran her tongue over a canine—"...bite."

"We'll see if our schedules match!" called Maribella as she ran away, with every intention of *not* visiting the Baroness anytime soon.

"Maribella!" called Baron Blauca as she dashed off the stage and pushed through the crowd. "Where are you going? You're going to miss the fireworks! They'll be going off any minute now!"

She ran as fast as her feet could take her. Out of the crowd and Peabush Square, past the line of llamas, down the street, past Clarence and back into the bookshop.

It was eerily silent.

The muffled sounds of the entire town in the midst of celebration were muted, and all the lights were out. The place was dark and quiet and felt abandoned. Nights before, it had been filled with people and life. Now it seemed like a place from a dream. A memory. Like Maribella was standing in yesterday but the entire world had moved on, and so she was there in the Cozy Quill alone and forgotten.

"Asteria!" she called, running through the first floor. She searched every aisle, every room. The main fireplace where they used to sit was cold and dead.

She took two stairs at a time and searched the second floor. She even climbed up the ladder to the reading nook tower to find it empty.

Oh, but it would have been a good place to watch the fireworks together, she thought as she climbed down.

Finally she burst into her own bedroom to find it empty.

There was a piece of paper on her bed.

There was writing on the paper.

She stepped forward and picked it up and read it.

I am leaving for the Ha-Mazan Tribes tonight. I can no longer fight against my fate. I must return to my Queen and devote my life to her. This is the only way.

Thank you for everything. Your Winter Solstice gift to me helped me write this note.

I am sorry for not saying goodbye. It would be too hard. This is better.

When I look at the stars, I will always think of you.

I will always love you.

Chapter 24

Gidget Leaves to Burn Things Down

Maribella sat on her bed for several minutes, alone in the dark, the note barely grasped between two fingers. There was a great emptiness inside her, as empty as the bookshop now was. Emptiness and regret.

I should have...I should have...

And then she heard a sound. It was a shuffling that came from downstairs.

Someone was in the shop.

She stuffed the note in a pocket and ran out her bedroom, across the second floor and down the stairs, hoping against hope.

She came back. She couldn't leave in the end. She came back for me.

Instead of a giant, she found quite the opposite. The diminutive Gidget the Goblin Girl was at a table fiddling with things. A stick sat on the table, and a checkered blanket was spread out with several objects collected on top.

"Gidget," said Maribella. "I didn't know you were here."

"Where else would I be?" said Gidget, meticulously going through the various objects. She checked a tin of cookies and then sealed it tight. The goblin no longer had her normal aura of extreme sleepiness, but now talked and moved with a casual and smooth confidence.

"Oh." Maribella ran a hand through hair, looking to the

display window. "Well I suppose I was just always used to you sleeping at the display. It's all you've ever done before. I didn't expect you to be up and about."

"Well I am now, and you won't be seeing much more of me either."

"Why do you say that?"

"Turns out I'll be following Asteria's example. New Year's Night is a good time to leave quietly. All you humans are busy drinking and throwing a right proper party. I thought I'd slip on out before you all wake up tomorrow."

Maribella blinked, taking in the scene. She just now realized the objects on the table were Gidget's traveling possessions. "You're leaving?"

"That I am."

"But...but why? I thought all you ever wanted to do was sleep. I thought you were the laziest individual in the whole world."

Gidget started tying the four corners of her blanket of possessions together. "Yep, that I was. A wonder, wasn't I? Still amazes me how uneducated some of you humans are about us goblins, though. We hibernate for half the year, and we rage in the wilderness for the other half."

"Rage?"

"That's right. Cause havoc and mischief, tear things down. It's what we do. We get all the eatin' and sleepin' out of the way all at once, then we go nuts."

"Oh. Well, I'm going to miss you. You really did help the shop."

"Yeah, I know I did. You had a really nice setup with the machine and all. What'd you call it again?"

She looked to the front window. "The Lagfa. Lever-Activated Goblin-Feeding Apparatus."

"Hah. Nice name, kid. Thank the Llama Merchant for me for that little invention."

Maribella was lost in her thoughts. Even as Gidget tied her bundle to the stick, she could only look down in silence.

"Sorry about Asteria leavin' you and all," said Gidget, as if sensing Maribella's sadness.

"Oh. Well. Yes. It's...it's no bother. There's nothing I can do about it, is there?"

"From my point of view, you could have done something."

Maribella looked up at the tiny goblin. "What?"

"You could have told her the truth."

"You mean tell her I love her?"

"Well. Yes. There's that. But I don't just mean that. I mean *all* the truth."

Maribella's eyes grew wide. "You know?"

Gidget shrugged. "Of course I do. It's pretty obvious to anyone paying attention, after all. What, you thought I wasn't listening to everything that was said in this place while sleeping on that display table? We goblins are multitaskers, we are. We can eat, sleep and listen all at the same time. And boy did I hear a lot. More than you did, it seems. For instance, old Clarence had to go and tell it to your face about him being sweet on the previous bookshop owner, didn't he? I called it when he knew where that stash of plates was kept back during the Pumpkin Festival."

She hefted her traveling stick with her bundle of goods onto her shoulder, then gave a casual salute. "*Welp.* I suppose I'm off. Be seein' you, kid. Don't go doing anything I wouldn't do. Maybe I'll come back in six months for my next hibernation. Yeah. Seems like a nice place." She began walking toward the door, waving over head. "I'm off to find my gang and burn stuff down. Maybe do my part for the species and push out a few pups. Goodbye, bookshop girl."

And just like that, Gidget was gone.

And then she stuck her head right back in.

"Oh yeah, one more thing," she said. "The road north out of town leads to the Ha-Mazan Tribes, for your information."

And *then* she was gone.

For a few heartbeats, Maribella stood alone in the bookshop.

And then she ran out the door and up the street.

Chapter 25

Maribella Tells the Truth

She ran against the flow of pedestrian traffic, traveling north on Main Street until she reached the edge of town, and then she kept going. Beyond were farmlands with patches of forests, and gentle slopes of hills. Everything was covered in snow and enveloped in darkness, the only light from the twinkling of stars overhead.

She ran until her lungs burned, and then she ran some more. The sounds of celebration fell far behind her until they completely disappeared. The world was black and silver and silent but for her own breath and the crunch of snow under her feet. She passed snow-covered trees and eventually came to the base of a hill.

Stopping there, Maribella looked back. Leafhaven was small now, filled with brilliant lights of all colors. It looked so very nice. So very comfortable. There was warmth back there, and friendship and a place to belong.

She turned back to the hill and forced her way up it. She knew after the crest, the town would no longer be visible.

Her calves burning, her feet growing numb with cold, her face flushed, her eyes moist, she finally reached the very top of the hill. It was dotted with a sparse amount of trees and a few rocks.

Asteria wasn't there.

And beyond, for miles and miles and miles, was only the

dark, dangerous wild.

I'm too late, she thought. *I'm too late.*

"You thought this would be good view for fireworks too, hmm?" came Asteria's voice.

Maribella looked about, finding the giant woman sitting on a rock at the edge of the road by a tree. She had completely missed her in the darkness. The sight of her brought new life to her body, and her lungs began working normally again.

"Asteria," she said.

"Bell."

For a few breaths, neither said a word.

"Why did you leave?" asked Maribella at length.

"I left note," said Asteria. "Did you not find note?"

"I found it." She brought it out, crumpled in her hand. "But that doesn't explain anything. Why did you leave?"

"Note explains all. I must defy fate no longer. I must follow fate's path for me. I must protect my Queen."

"But why didn't you tell me? Why did you just leave like this?"

"Because." Asteria stood up, walking the distance to Maribella but keeping a few steps away. "It would be too hard. You would cry, as you are doing now."

"Yes, I would."

"And now you have chased me down. Now you have come to try to tell me to not leave. But this is not a possible thing. I cannot go against fate. I know that you do not believe in this, but you must understand that I do. I cannot live knowing I have defied fate. You cannot change my mind."

Maribella shook her head. "No, that's not why I chased you down. I'm not here to change your mind."

"Oh? Is this so?"

"It is."

"Then why have you run here in such a huff?"

"To finally tell you the truth."

"And what truth is this?"

"I'm not who I say I am." She lifted her chin, meeting

Asteria's eyes with her own focused, watery ones. "My name is not Maribella Waters."

A calm wind blew across the top of the hill. The silence of the countryside at night fell on the two women like gentle snow.

"What is this you speak of?" said Asteria, her voice very small.

"I'm not from the border villages of Fraey Tarta, like you guessed. I lied to you when I said I was."

"Why did you make this lie?"

"Because nobody could know the truth. Not even you. That man who was at the bookshop the other day, the one who grabbed me. I *do* know him. He's not a stranger. He's a knight of Fraey Tarta."

Asteria stood silent.

Maribella felt tears welling up in her eyes, and she sniffed, forcing her voice to not shake. "There are many who would not understand my decision. There are many who would even judge me harshly. After all, when you just look at what I did on the surface, it looks horrible. I ran away, just as Fraey Tarta was being invaded."

Asteria stood silent.

"But few would understand. I think Lady Malicent would. I learned that, in the end of all things. She grew up trapped and in a prison as well. Only in my case, I was traded off. Sold, really. To a horrible man I had no love for. A man quick to anger. And so we married. And my future was one I couldn't bare. It was one of being trapped, and fated to give birth to heir after heir."

Asteria stood silent.

"And so I couldn't do it. I made plans to escape. I corresponded with Leafhaven to purchase the Cozy Quill. I ran away. I came here. On my own, in secret, using a fake identity. I didn't know how it would turn out, but it turned out greater than I could have imagined. I never thought I would have met someone like you, but then I did. And well, now, here I am."

Asteria took a single step forward. "Bell, what is it you are telling me?"

Maribella swallowed. "The rumors we've all been hearing," she said. "How the Queen of Fraey Tarta has been deathly ill, how she's been confined, how she probably won't make it. That story was just a cover for the truth."

"The truth."

"Yes, the truth that I can finally say aloud. The truth that I can no longer hide. I am Lady Regina Emeralda, Queen of Fraey Tarta."

She tensed, wondering how Asteria would take the revelation.

Asteria's head dropped, her face hidden.

"All this time," she said, her voice low and quiet. "All this time, here in Leafhaven, I thought I was running away from my fate."

In the distance, colorful fireworks began popping in the night sky.

When Asteria looked up, tears streamed down her cheeks. The firework colors played against her face—green, red, yellow, blue, purple.

"But in reality, I was running *toward* my fate."

She dropped to one knee suddenly and placed her hands on her thigh, then bowed her head.

"My Queen," she said. "Would you allow me the honor of devoting my life to you, of protecting you against all dangers, of being by your side at all times?"

She lifted her head, and there was only love in her eyes.

"Will you allow me my fate?"

Maribella's heart twisted in her chest. She burst into tears and jumped into Asteria's arms, embracing her. They held each other for a long time as fireworks exploded in the distance over Leafhaven, crying into each other, the heat of their bodies warming them in the cold night.

"Yes, yes, and forever yes. I love you," said Maribella.

"I love you," said Asteria. "My Queen. My fate."

And they kissed, holding each other on that hilltop for as long as the fireworks went off.

It was an especially long fireworks show that year.

Chapter 26

Maribella Finally Hears the Punchline

Maribella and Asteria made the long journey home hand-in-hand from the snowy hilltop back to Leafhaven and down Main Street. The fireworks ended, but there were still plenty of people about.

They came across the child who liked to chase his hoop with his stick all day and he stopped in front of them. You may remember him from when Maribella first arrived in town and she needed help with directions. He was very unhelpful.

"Oh no," said Maribella, frowning at the child. "It's *him*."

"Who is this boy-child?" asked Asteria.

"He's a horrible boy-child who is of no substance or help whatsoever. And he's prone to telling terrible jokes that make absolutely no sense and have no punchline or any semblance of humor."

"Tra la la!" the child sang. "I have a joke for you."

Maribella groaned. "Oh, very well. Hurry up and get on with it so we can be on our way."

"Two fine fellows stood atop a tall bridge. One held a parrot on his arm, the other held a pipe in his hand. The first fellow said, 'My parrot with catch anything that is thrown into the air.' The second fellow immediately tossed his pipe over the edge of the bridge, and the parrot flew off and down below. When the parrot came back to his master, why, what was it he had in his talons?"

Maribella groaned even louder. "The second fellow's pipe, of course."

"Wrong! The parrot had the brick! Tra la la!"

The boy ran away with his hoop and stick.

As Maribella stood there, staring off into the void, reality itself lost all meaning. She wasn't standing on Main Street in Leafhaven in the cold, she was cast across the cosmos to tumble forever through time and space.

"The brick..." she said, eyes opening wide. "The parrot had the brick...in his hands..."

"Bell," said Asteria, arching a brow. "Have you gone mind-sick?"

Maribella turned to Asteria, and suddenly grabbed her by the shirt, staring deeply into her eyes. "It was the brick. The *brick!* The parrot had the *brick!* From the other man! From...from...*from months ago!* Oh my *God!* It wasn't two jokes! It was one joke! One joke the entire time! He waited months...months I say! He held the punchline this entire time!"

"Brick? What do you speak of? This joke makes no sense to me."

Maribella began to violently shake Asteria by the shirt. "But don't you see? It was from the man standing underneath the bridge! The man building a house with bricks. He had one leftover brick. He threw his leftover brick up into the air. And then the parrot caught it. Because the parrot will catch anything you throw into the air. And you thought it was going to be the pipe. But it wasn't! The man threw the brick into the air! All these months! It was the brick, Asteria! It was the brick! This is the punchline! This is finally the punchline!"

"There, there," said Asteria, calmly picking Maribella up and placing her over a shoulder like a sack of potatoes. "It has been long and exciting day for us all. You need rest. I will now proceed to carry you to bed."

"The brick!" cackled Maribella like a madwoman as she was carried off into town. "It was the brick!"

Chapter 27

The Reader Takes the Final Quiz

Yes, that's you. An entire chapter, named after you. How often does *that* happen? You're practically a main character in this story by now.

And so as we draw close to the ending of our tale, it is time for the final interactive portion of the book, the last quiz. Everything you have read up until now has culminated in one single question that will truly test if you've been paying attention or not. This final exam is worth one hundred percent of your score (the first two quizzes were just warm-ups).

You also have a personal guarantee that this quiz will not be a trick question, like the first two quizzes. It is multiple choice, with three options, and the answer is one of the three options. I promise. No sneaky tricks whatsoever.

The question is this:

Of all the authors mentioned in this book, who is the greatest one?

A) Isambard Ruskin

B) Robert Airickson R. R. R. Branderstopper

C) Eustace Hemingwoh

Take your time, now. Think long and hard about it. You can't rush these things.

Have you decided? Is your answer locked in? All right, then.

The answer is none of the above. It was another trick

question. Sir Edmundus Gloopinbottom is the greatest author mentioned in this book.

He won't show up again, because his overpowering character would take away from the heart of this story. But just know he was there, all along, at the Winter Solstice party, at the New Year's Night celebration, and stayed in town for quite a while before setting off for the horizon and more adventures.

Chapter 28

Maribella and Asteria Read a Happy Ending

In the following weeks, Maribella learned that the King of Fraey Tarta announced the death of Queen Regina Emeralda, which was a perfectly fine thing to announce as far as Maribella was concerned. She could only assume that the knight of Fraey Tarta had told the King what Maribella had done, and in the face of such a profound and elaborate show of rejection, the King simply threw up his hands and wrote Maribella off. He would probably remarry very soon.

Maribella and Asteria were the happiest they had ever been in those days after New Year's Night. They ran the bookshop together, and nobody else in town ever learned of Maribella's true regal identity. She curtsied to Baron and Baroness Blauca as well as Lady Malicent whenever she saw them, and only she and Asteria were aware that if Maribella had never made her life choice, it was *them* that should have been bowing to *her*, had they ever met. Maribella was just fine with the change.

A couple weeks into the new year, Maribella and Asteria found themselves cuddled together up in their reading nook tower finishing a book. It was a quiet evening of silver light as thick layers of fallen snow reflected the moon. The fire crackled peacefully and the town was asleep.

Reading together was now better than ever for Maribella. Before, they were two friends sitting next to each other. Now they could entwine themselves, and things were much more comfortable that way.

The book they were finishing was a short one called *The Dragonslayer's Courtship*. It was about a roaming knight who found himself in a small, quaint village, and he came across the most beautiful woman he had ever seen. She was a dyer, for the forest the village was next to was quite famous for its beautiful purple flowers.

Upon seeing the dyer woman, the knight proclaimed she was so stunning that she couldn't be of this world. She was too gorgeous, too graceful, too perfect. He stayed in the small village and courted her for many weeks, and after spending time with her his first assumption was solidified in his mind. The dyer woman was downright angelic. And what's more, the dyer woman seemed to be quite taken with him. He couldn't believe it. Even though this knight was an all around agreeable fellow with plenty of virtue, industriousness, and not to mention good looks, he simply couldn't accept that a woman of this quality would ever consider him for a husband.

And so he announced that he wanted nothing more than to marry her, but he also claimed it was impossible for her to take a man like him as a husband, even though he was an accomplished knight of the realm. He needed to do something *great* for her to marry him.

Rumors were that a dragon had been terrorizing the countryside, flying over villages and stealing sheep before going back to its cave upon a mountain. The cave was close by to the dyer woman's village, so the love-struck knight promised he would set out to slay the dragon and not come back until he had done so, and only then would he feel worthy enough for his maiden's hand.

And so he set out. Donning armor and shield and sword, he ventured into the dragon's lair, where he was soundly trounced. The dragon flung him out, and he crawled back to the village only slightly charred.

The next time he brought a large arbalest. "Surely this

missile will penetrate its scales," he claimed as he crept into the cave.

It did not. The knight was once again thrown out of the cave to the great and booming laughter of the dragon.

Then he thought up the bright idea to hire help. He spent much coin on a group of traveling mercenaries to back him up in the fight. The mercenaries ran at first sight of the dragon. Once again, the knight had failed.

Again and again he tried, and nothing worked. Magical tomes and potions did nothing. Blessed armor might as well have been cursed. Torches and fire bombs only seemed to comfort the beast. Poison was like candy to it. Prayers to deities above went unanswered.

He tried for one entire year, and at the end of that year, he came back to the dyer woman completely defeated.

"I cannot do it," he said. "I cannot defeat the dragon. I am not enough, my love. I am not worthy."

"Oh, dearest knight," said the dyer woman. "I've been trying to tell you again and again. You are enough. You are worthy. Not because you defeated a dragon or not, but because of the love you hold in your heart for me, and the love I hold for you. Because of the way I feel safe when you are around. Because of the way you make me laugh when you jest. Because of the ache in my chest when you are not here. I never wanted a dead dragon, I only wanted a man who cared, who loved, and who was there."

At the end of the book, the two of them got married. The final line was somewhat of a cliché one, but Maribella smiled as she read it. She always thought it was a perfect way to end a good book, even if it was a little well-used by this point.

Warm and comfortable in a place she loved more than anywhere else, next to a person she loved more than anyone else, Maribella got to the very last page of the book, and read the very last line of the page.

"And they lived happily ever after."

Epilogue

"**A**nd then what?" asked Asteria.

Maribella looked up. "What do you mean?"

Asteria gave a light shrug. "And then what happened?"

"Nothing happened. That's the end of the book. That's the last line."

"Nothing happened after that? They just stood there frozen for all of time?"

Maribella laughed. "Of course not. That would be silly. It's implied that they went on living their lives, happily ever after. See? It says right there."

"Yes, but what did they do?"

"They lived life."

"Yes, but did anything else important happen?"

Maribella put the book aside and narrowed her eyes, giving Asteria a hard look. "What do you mean?"

"I mean what I say. Did anything else important happen?"

"Well, it might have."

"So why did author not mention it? Why did book not keep going after this last chapter?"

Maribella sighed. "If it was something really important and related to the story, then the book wouldn't have ended there. There would have been another chapter. The book would keep going until all the important things related to the story were covered. That's how novels work."

"Yes, but what if something important *not* related to the

story happened?"

"*Not* related to the story?"

"Yes, an event that involved them, and is very important, but not directly related to their story."

"Well that's what sequels are for. Sequels are another story with the same characters."

"Is there a sequel to this book?"

"No."

"Will one ever be written?"

"I don't believe so."

"Then how do we know?"

"Know what?"

"That something big and important did not happen after this last chapter?"

Maribella sighed again and rubbed her forehead. "Something big and important?"

Asteria stroked at her chin, looking away and thinking deeply, apparently. "Yes. What if a big, important, notable event happened after the story, after the last chapter, but it was not directly related to the story at hand, but it was still a very important event worth mentioning, possibly for future story?"

Maribella nodded. "Okay. So, you're asking, what if a big, important, notable event happened after the story, after the last chapter, but it wasn't anything actually related to the story you just read, but it's still a very important event worth mentioning because it might be related to another story?"

"Yes. What if that?"

Maribella thought about it for a minute.

She turned to Asteria and gave a great, big shrug.

"Well, in that case, I suppose the author would write an epilogue."

Lightning flashed and crackled inside the room, and loud booming clashes rang out. Wind lashed at their hair and sent the book and blanket on them flying. Both women covered their eyes in total blinding confusion, wondering how a storm had managed to find its way inside their cozy little reading nook tower.

When the flashes of light and sounds and wind finally passed, they opened their eyes to find a small young woman standing in the room by the window.

Maribella jumped with a little yelp and instinctively threw the wooden pig carving that Edgar the pig farmer had given her.

(*Hah!* I bet you thought I forgot all about that wooden pig carving! Well I didn't! I told you its backstory was going to be important all the way back in chapter one, and now you know why!)

The pig hit the strange young woman right in the head and she grunted and winced and held her forehead. "Wha...did you...did you throw a rock at me?"

"It was a pig," said Maribella.

"Oh no," said the young woman as she took stock of her surroundings and looked at Maribella and Asteria. There was a confused and slightly frightened tone to her voice. "More weird people."

"I *beg your pardon,*" said Maribella, unable to let go of Asteria. "Who are you and how did you get in this room?"

The young woman was quite strange. She looked like she had been roughing it in the wild for a bit, or perhaps lived on a farm that wasn't doing quite so well. She wore a dirty brown burlap dress and she had black hair. She had a mighty hump on her back which made her stoop downward, and there was also some small deformities in her hands and face as well, although her eyes were quite striking. On one hand she wore a strange gauntlet made of something that looked like glass or crystal or even diamond, and little flashes of different colored lights flickered on it.

She looked about her surroundings and seemed just as confused as Maribella felt. "Where am I now?" she asked. "Oh, this isn't good for my anxiety issues. What is this place? What, it's all snowy outside now?"

Maribella and Asteria looked at each other. "Uh, snowy? It's been snowing for weeks."

"No it hasn't," said the strange woman. "It's been sunny. I was about to die so I reached in the bag and thought of something that would take me far away, and when I pulled my hand out this weird dumb gauntlet was stuck on me. Then there was a bright flash and when it went away I was in some spooky old haunted house with a bunch of weird people staring at me. It was raining and thundering outside and there was a moose head on the wall. Then I pushed one of these lights on the gauntlet and now it's all cold and snowy and I'm in some weird cozy room with a couple lesbians."

Maribella and Asteria could do nothing but blink.

"Beatrix?" shouted the strange woman into the air. "Beatrix, are you here? Oh, but what do I do now?" She suddenly closed her eyes tightly. "All right. It's magic, not technology. *Intention*. Come on, it's *intention* that makes magic work. That's what Beatrix said. Okay, magic glove, take me back home."

She slapped her hand on the gauntlet. More blinding flashes of light flickered all around her along with wind and loud pops, and when it was all over, the strange young woman was gone.

Now, dear reader, you might be confused at this point. But you see, so were Maribella and Asteria, so you know exactly how they felt at the time. In fact, I'm confused as well. We're all confused together. The story of the magically appearing and disappearing strange young woman with the magic gauntlet and a mighty hump on her back was spread all over town. As time went by, people just assumed that it would one day be explained. But it never was. The young woman never appeared again, and there were no reports from the lands abroad of anything similar happening.

But it was important, Maribella was absolutely certain of that, so it was put down on these pages for your reading pleasure.

Eventually, as the weeks went by, and the months went by, and the years went by, everybody completely forgot about the strange young woman.

Maribella and Asteria lived out their lives together in love and happiness. People came to town, people left town. Babies were born and grew into children who were eager to buy up new copies of the *Lady Jeanie Mysteries* books. Duckovers came and went, along with Pumpkin Festivals and Winter Solstices. Leafhaven thrived.

One day, Clarence was no longer the oldest man in town. He was celebrated on that day, as all loved ones should be.

Maribella became fast friends with Lady Malicent, and it was the most unexpected of friendships. They bonded over their love of reading, and traded books to each other to talk about later. Instead of crowded, overpriced tenements, she built an orphanage for lost and unwanted children on the land the Baron offered. It was said in town that she had forgotten her empathy once she had stopped reading years ago, and found it when she began reading again. After all, every time you read a book, you see the world from the eyes of another person, and that, of course, is the basis for all empathy.

Baron Blauca proved an admirable community leader, something that is all too often rare these days. Maribella never did quite find out if his wife was actually a vampiress or not. To this day, nobody has ever seen the woman in the sun.

Catalina the Llama Merchant, Dave, the llamas, and Esteban the sloth would often visit on their merchant trips through the land. Catalina and Dave got married one day and even had a little baby tucked away like a grub worm and tied to the front of Dave. Maribella was quite cross with them that they hadn't decided to marry in Leafhaven where they met, but such is life.

Captain Hargle was fired from his position as Captain of the Town Guard because he was caught sleeping one too many times. He was hired by his twin brother Captain Bargle to be the first mate on his boat, and to this very day they still fight in only the way brothers can.

One day, Mr Reginald Cumberbutton and Ms Henrietta Appletop left town, proclaiming they were going to see the world. The last anyone heard is they made it as far as the apple tree on the hill outside town and are currently touring the apples.

Every year for six months, Gidget the Goblin Girl hibernated at the Cozy Quill Bookshop. It was always a time of eager anticipation for the town, and she was fed much food via the Lever-Activated Goblin Feeding Apparatus whenever she began her sleep.

The Ha-Mazan Tribes never tried invading south again, and the borderlands were safe. Many of the Ha-Mazan citizens actually became great merchant traders, and they became known far and wide for the high quality tables they sold.

As for Maribella and Asteria? They grew old together. They would always look back on the events of this story with a great sense of nostalgia, and just a bit of painful longing. They were good days. Days worth writing down.

The bookshop thrived, and Asteria became a great reader just like Maribella. Do you have a local bookshop in your town, perhaps? Have you been to it lately? I would give the advice to pay it a visit. Bookshops are magical places, after all, full of wonder and possibility. It would also make the bookshop owner very happy for you to visit, and put a smile on his or her face.

I would also give the advice to read more, and to read with people, as well. A loved one. A mother, a father, a grandparent. It can simply be a friend, if need be. If they claim they dislike reading, then what if they simply haven't been offered anything that interests them? You may be surprised.

And if you have no friends, then you can always make one over a book. We all love books, and someone that loves something you love is a friend.

After all, that's how it worked for Maribella and Asteria.

And where are they now?

To this day, they are living happily ever after.

A Note From The Author

Dearest Reader,

Congratulations.
You made it to the end.
I certainly hope you enjoyed reading this book as much as I enjoyed writing it. If not, I deeply apologize.

I feel like I should say a few words about *The Bookshop and the Barbarian* because of how wildly different it is from my usual publications. Everything I write falls under the umbrella of fantasy, but my previous work is all much grimmer and darker and full of people stabbing or shooting each other. Imagine if Asteria never found Maribella and she went wild with her greataxe.

So why did I write *The Bookshop and the Barbarian* if I usually prefer books with far more killings and mayhem? Well, I like different stuff. So yes, I enjoy feel-good, uplifting, cozy, slice-of-life fantasy. Or at least I needed to get it out of my system between books that include a lot more dismembering. I wanted to write something positive and happy and warm, and also something that celebrates books, friends, and the fall and winter seasons.

So that's what I did. There will probably be a mix of books in the future for me. And if you're a gentle reader with a delicate disposition, I suggest you not dive into my backlist of books. But if you don't mind a good bloody murder or two, by all means take a peek, and who knows, you might even come across a certain world-hopping strange young woman with a hump on her back.

If you want, you can leave a review of *The Bookshop and the Barbarian* on its Amazon page. Like Maribella's addiction to reading books, authors are sustained by reviews.

And if you'd like, you can follow my Amazon author page to get notifications for future releases, found in the following link:

https://www.amazon.com/Morgan-Stang/e/ B086CYW193

Thanks and Keep Reading,
Morgan Stang

Printed in Great Britain
by Amazon

44726421R00118